V. S. NAIPAUL

Miguel Street

PICADOR

First published 1959 by André Deutsch

First published by Picador 2002 in an omnibus edition with *The Mystic Masseur*

This edition published with a new preface 2011 by Picador
an imprint of Pan Macmillan
20 New Wharf Road, London N1 9RR
Associated companies throughout the world
www.panmacmillan.com

ISBN 978-0-330-52300-4

9 8

A CIP catalogue record for this book is available from
the British Library.

Typeset by Intype London Ltd
Printed and bound in Great Britain by
CPI Group (UK) Ltd., Croydon, CR0 4YY

Preface

THE STORIES IN *Miguel Street* were begun by a man who had everything to learn about writing and himself. The writing ambition had come very early to me, but it had always been only a kind of warm glow inside me, giving me the vaguest idea of what I might do. The writing ambition had come without the wish to do a particular kind of book, and so it stayed for years. I didn't even know in the beginning what kind of writer I might be. Was my gift a comic one or was it profounder? I wrote many stories in this blank period, but nothing like a book announced itself to me. I did attempt a book; I attempted two books; but the creative fog refused to lift. The first book I attempted was a version of *Black Mischief*, giving it a Trinidadian setting. I managed, with a kind of self-induced blindness, to take this to the end in the long vacation, writing very fast when the end was in sight. One man said it was 'phoney Waugh'. I suffered at that, and marked this man down both for his wit and the soundness of his judgement. I believe the book was actually presented, by a very kind friend, to a London publisher, but fortunately for everyone it was turned down.

It seemed to me as a result that farce or comedy was not what I was meant for, and the next book I attempted three or four years later was extremely serious. I had no story; I thought I should do an account of a day in the life of someone such as I had been. The book lumbered on and on. When I left Oxford I took this dreadful half-book with me to London. I had had the good fortune to land a little editorial job at the BBC. This job not only saved me from destitution; it also put me in touch with real writers and real critics, and I had the folly or the vanity to send my manuscript to one of those people. He sent it back almost by return post and said that I should forget this work. It was very wounding to me; especially as it was so close to what I had begun to feel about the book. And it was with this great depression, of rejection and general hopelessness, that one afternoon, in the freelancers' room in the Langham Hotel, then a part of the BBC, I sat before one of the big typewriters and started the first story of *Miguel Street*. I had no idea where I was going, but somehow the idea had come to me that I should not leave the freelancers' room until I had finished the story. My life as a writer until then had been full of beginnings, and it would have added to my gloom to make yet another false start.

The next day I began and finished a second story, and the day after that I did a third. These stories had the same imaginative setting, were written in the same tone of voice, in the same spare language, and were in fact part of a vision I didn't know I possessed as a writer until the moment of writing. After a few days – of immense excitement – the stories became too long to be completed at a sitting. The stories had to be carried in my head until the following day, and sometimes for days. It was new to me to carry work with me for many days; and without my knowing it, without understanding what I had let myself in for I in this way learnt something about the nature of writing. The reader of this book can follow this process of learning and discovery in the stories of *Miguel Street* sequence. He may think I claim too much for the stories, but I am speaking here of something very personal, something that tipped me over from despair into beginning to be a writer.

This is a process that happened in my own mind and will not be easy to explain. Until I had begun *Miguel Street* I had been obsessed with style and language, and had worked very hard to master that aspect of the craft. I had read and tried to learn from many of the approved masters, Defoe, Swift, Dryden and even a few of the moderns who had come my way – the now-forgotten H. M. Tomlinson among them. I suppose they all helped in a way, but they didn't take me nearer to becoming a writer. They didn't take me nearer into understanding what my material was going to be. In fact they made it harder for me to have an idea of the value of my own material; their metropolitan glamour was too great.

The *Miguel Street* stories seemed to write themselves. I didn't step back to consider myself writing, and it was hard for me to understand where I had got that tone of voice. Many years later I thought the voice came from the Castilian, and especially from the sixteenth-century picaresque novel, *Lazarillo de Tormes*. I had studied and greatly admired this book in the sixth form. Later I was to translate it. I was hoping that the Penguin Classics might want to do it; but after a little initial encouragement it was not to be. But the effect of all this was that the tone of the old Spanish book sang in my head, and I am sure it helped me to get started.

The stories I was writing in this dreamlike way were of the life of a Port of Spain street. I had no idea where the stories would lead me and the theme of the street and its life was part of the luck of that occasion in the freelancers' room in the BBC. I had worried a great deal about arriving at my material. This luck undid that worry. To write about the street, which I of course knew, was to be flooded with material, an embarrassment of riches, folk myths, folk songs, newspaper stories, all worked on now by transforming memory. My concern when I began had been with language, a wish to raise my language above the language of the school essay, and to turn it into something closer to the writing one might come upon in a book. Yet, miraculously this concern with language led to narrative, to writing at length. It led me very close to having an idea of the book. I had begun, as I said, to carry the material in my head, and insensibly the stories became longer. I didn't know where I was going. The story of 'The Enemy' was written as a part of *Miguel Street*. At this stage

I was sufficiently in control of my material to understand that it was wrong for the *Street*. I kept it apart, then and later, and I was glad that I did so because three years later it led me to one of the stronger scenes of a much more important book, *A House for Mr Biswas*. To have used the material in another way would have been to lose it. So I was given a sense of what I was doing and was no longer as keen as I might have been earlier to bulk out a book. Inevitably the stories of *Miguel Street* came to an end; it became important to look for a publisher.

In a better-ordered world the stories of *Miguel Street* would have excited a publisher. The publisher I was dealing with was indeed excited; he wanted to publish me, but he had the publisher's wisdom about short stories. He said that they never sold. He wanted a novel before anything else and so I spent the rest of the year trying to write a novel. It was four years before *Miguel Street* was published, and – alas for the publisher's wisdom – it has never been out of print, earning its regular fifty per cent for the publisher. The stories that were done later need no apology; I consider them part of my work.

For my Mother and Kamla

Contents

1. Bogart

EVERY MORNING WHEN he got up Hat would sit on the banister of his back verandah and shout across, 'What happening there, Bogart?'

Bogart would turn in his bed and mumble softly, so that no one heard, 'What happening there, Hat?'

It was something of a mystery why he was called Bogart; but I suspect that it was Hat who gave him the name. I don't know if you remember the year the film *Casablanca* was made. That was the year when Bogart's fame spread like fire through Port of Spain and hundreds of young men began adopting the hard-boiled Bogartian attitude.

Before they called him Bogart they called him Patience, because he played that game from morn till night. Yet he never liked cards.

Whenever you went over to Bogart's little room you found him sitting on his bed with the cards in seven lines on a small table in front of him.

'What happening there, man?' he would ask quietly, and then he would say nothing for ten or fifteen minutes. And somehow you felt you couldn't really talk to Bogart, he looked so bored and superior. His eyes were small and sleepy. His face was fat and his hair was gleaming black. His arms were plump. Yet he was not a funny man. He did everything with a captivating languor. Even when he licked his thumb to deal out the cards there was grace in it.

He was the most bored man I ever knew.

He made a pretence of making a living by tailoring, and he had even paid me some money to write a sign for him:

TAILOR AND CUTTER
Suits made to Order
Popular and Competitive Prices

He bought a sewing-machine and some blue and white and brown chalks. But I never could imagine him competing with any-one; and I cannot remember him making a suit. He was a little bit like Popo, the carpenter next door, who never made a stick of furniture, and was always planing and chiselling and making what I think he called mortises. Whenever I asked him, 'Mr Popo, what you making?' he would reply, 'Ha, boy! That's the question. I making the thing without a name.' Bogart was never even making anything like this.

Being a child, I never wondered how Bogart came by any money. I assumed that grown-ups had money as a matter of course. Popo had a wife who worked at a variety of jobs; and ended up by becoming the friend of many men. I could never think of Bogart as having mother or father; and he never brought a woman to his little room. This little room of his was called the servant-room but no servant to the people in the main house ever lived there. It was just an architectural convention.

It is still something of a miracle to me that Bogart managed to make friends. Yet he did make many friends; he was at one time quite the most popular man in the street. I used to see him squatting on the pavement with all the big men of the street. And while Hat or Edward or Eddoes was talking, Bogart would just look down and draw rings with his fingers on the pavement. He never laughed audibly. He never told a story. Yet whenever there was a fête or something like that, everybody would say, 'We must have Bogart.

He smart like hell, that man.' In a way he gave them great solace and comfort, I suppose.

And so every morning, as I told you, Hat would shout, very loudly, 'What happening there, Bogart?'

And he would wait for the indeterminate grumble which was Bogart saying, 'What happening there, Hat?'

But one morning, when Hat shouted, there was no reply. Something which had appeared unalterable was missing.

Bogart had vanished; had left us without a word.

The men in the street were silent and sorrowful for two whole days. They assembled in Bogart's little room. Hat lifted up the deck of cards that lay on Bogart's table and dropped two or three cards at a time reflectively.

Hat said, 'You think he gone Venezuela?'

But no one knew. Bogart told them so little.

And the next morning Hat got up and lit a cigarette and went to his back verandah and was on the point of shouting, when he remembered. He milked the cows earlier than usual that morning, and the cows didn't like it.

A month passed; then another month. Bogart didn't return.

Hat and his friends began using Bogart's room as their club-house. They played *wappee* and drank rum and smoked, and sometimes brought the odd stray woman to the room. Hat was presently involved with the police for gambling and sponsoring cock-fighting; and he had to spend a lot of money to bribe his way out of trouble.

It was as if Bogart had never come to Miguel Street. And after all Bogart had been living in the street only for four years or so. He had come one day with a single suitcase, looking for a room, and he had spoken to Hat who was squatting outside his gate, smoking a cigarette and reading the cricket scores in the evening paper. Even then he hadn't said much. All he said – that was Hat's story – was, 'You know any rooms?' and Hat had led him to the next yard where there was this furnished servant-room going for eight dollars a month. He had installed himself there immediately, brought out a pack of cards, and begun playing patience.

This impressed Hat.

For the rest he had always remained a man of mystery. He became Patience.

When Hat and everybody else had forgotten or nearly forgotten Bogart, he returned. He turned up one morning just about seven and found Eddoes had a woman on his bed. The woman jumped up and screamed. Eddoes jumped up, not so much afraid as embarrassed.

Bogart said, 'Move over. I tired and I want to sleep.'

He slept until five that afternoon, and when he woke up he found his room full of the old gang. Eddoes was being very loud and noisy to cover up his embarrassment. Hat had brought a bottle of rum.

Hat said, 'What happening there, Bogart?'

And he rejoiced when he found his cue taken up. 'What happening there, Hat?'

Hat opened the bottle of rum, and shouted to Boyee to go buy a bottle of soda water.

Bogart asked, 'How the cows, Hat?'

'They all right.'

'And Boyee?'

'He all right too. Ain't you just hear me call him?'

'And Errol?'

'He all right too. But what happening, Bogart? *You* all right?'

Bogart nodded, and drank a long Madrassi shot of rum. Then another, and another; and they had presently finished the bottle.

'Don't worry,' Bogart said. 'I go buy another.'

They had never seen Bogart drink so much; they had never heard him talk so much; and they were alarmed. No one dared to ask Bogart where he had been.

Bogart said, 'You boys been keeping my room hot all the time.'

'It wasn't the same without you,' Hat replied.

But they were all worried. Bogart was hardly opening his lips when he spoke. His mouth was twisted a little, and his accent was getting slightly American.

'Sure, sure,' Bogart said, and he had got it right. He was just like an actor.

Hat wasn't sure that Bogart was drunk.

In appearance, you must know, Hat recalled Rex Harrison, and he had done his best to strengthen the resemblance. He combed his hair backwards, screwed up his eyes, and he spoke very nearly like Harrison.

'Damn it, Bogart,' Hat said, and he became very like Rex Harrison. 'You may as well tell us everything right away.'

Bogart showed his teeth and laughed in a twisted, cynical way.

'Sure I'll tell,' he said, and got up and stuck his thumbs inside his waistband. 'Sure, I'll tell everything.'

He lit a cigarette, leaned back in such a way that the smoke got into his eyes; and, squinting, he drawled out his story.

He had got a job on a ship and had gone to British Guiana. There he had deserted, and gone into the interior. He became a cowboy on the Rupununi, smuggled things (he didn't say what) into Brazil, and had gathered some girls from Brazil and taken them to Georgetown. He was running the best brothel in the town when the police treacherously took his bribes and arrested him.

'It was a high-class place,' he said, 'no bums. Judges and doctors and big shot civil servants.'

'What happen?' Eddoes asked. 'Jail?'

'How you so stupid?' Hat said. 'Jail, when the man here with we. But why you people so stupid? Why you don't let the man talk?'

But Bogart was offended, and refused to speak another word.

*

From then on the relationship between these men changed. Bogart became the Bogart of the films. Hat became Harrison. And the morning exchange became this:

'Bogart!'

'Shaddup, Hat!'

Bogart now became the most feared man in the street. Even Big Foot was said to be afraid of him. Bogart drank and swore and gambled with the best. He shouted rude remarks at girls walking by themselves in the street. He bought a hat, and pulled down the brim over his eyes. He became a regular sight, standing against the high concrete fence of his yard, hands in his pockets, one foot jammed against the wall, and an eternal cigarette in his mouth.

Then he disappeared again. He was playing cards with the gang in his room, and he got up and said, 'I'm going to the latrine.'

They didn't see him for four months.

When he returned, he had grown a little fatter but he had become a little more aggressive. His accent was now pure American. To complete the imitation, he began being expansive towards children. He called out to them in the streets, and gave them money to buy gum and chocolate. He loved stroking their heads, and giving them good advice.

The third time he went away and came back he gave a great party in his room for all the children or kids, as he called them. He bought cases of Solo and Coca-Cola and Pepsi-Cola and about a bushel of cakes.

Then Sergeant Charles, the policeman who lived up Miguel Street at number forty-five, came and arrested Bogart.

'Don't act tough, Bogart,' Sergeant Charles said.

But Bogart failed to take the cue.

'What happening, man? I ain't do anything.'

Sergeant Charles told him.

There was a little stir in the papers. The charge was bigamy;

but it was up to Hat to find out all the inside details that the news-papers never mention.

'You see,' Hat said on the pavement that evening, 'the man leave his first wife in Tunapuna and come to Port of Spain. They couldn't have children. He remain here feeling sad and small. He go away, find a girl in Caroni and he give she a baby. In Caroni they don't make joke about that sort of thing and Bogart had to get married to the girl.'

'But why he leave she?' Eddoes asked.

'To be a man, among we men.'

2. The Thing Without a Name

THE ONLY THING that Popo, who called himself a carpenter, ever built was the little galvanized-iron workshop under the mango tree at the back of his yard. And even that he didn't quite finish. He couldn't be bothered to nail on the sheets of galvanized-iron for the roof, and kept them weighted down with huge stones. Whenever there was a high wind the roof made a frightening banging noise and seemed ready to fly away.

And yet Popo was never idle. He was always busy hammering and sawing and planing. I liked watching him work. I liked the smell of the woods – cyp and cedar and crapaud. I liked the colour of the shavings, and I liked the way the sawdust powdered Popo's kinky hair.

'What you making, Mr Popo?' I asked.

Popo would always say, 'Ha, boy! That's the question. I making the thing without a name.'

I liked Popo for that. I thought he was a poetic man.

One day I said to Popo, 'Give me something to make.'

'What you want to make?' he said.

It was hard to think of something I really wanted.

'You see,' Popo said. 'You thinking about the thing without a name.'

Eventually I decided on an egg-stand.

'Who you making it for?' Popo asked.

'Ma.'

[8]

He laughed. 'Think she going use it?'

My mother was pleased with the egg-stand, and used it for about a week. Then she seemed to forget all about it; and began putting the eggs in bowls or plates, just as she did before.

And Popo laughed when I told him. He said, 'Boy, the only thing to make is the thing without a name.'

After I painted the tailoring sign for Bogart, Popo made me do one for him as well.

He took the little red stump of a pencil he had stuck over his ear and puzzled over the words. At first he wanted to announce himself as an architect; but I managed to dissuade him. He wasn't sure about the spelling. The finished sign said:

BUILDER AND CONTRACTOR
Carpenter
And Cabinet-Maker

And I signed my name, as sign-writer, in the bottom right-hand corner.

Popo liked standing up in front of the sign. But he had a little panic when people who didn't know about him came to inquire.

'The carpenter fellow?' Popo would say. 'He don't live here again.'

I thought Popo was a much nicer man than Bogart. Bogart said little to me; but Popo was always ready to talk. He talked about serious things, like life and death and work, and I felt he really liked talking to me.

Yet Popo was not a popular man in the street. They didn't think he was mad or stupid. Hat used to say, 'Popo too conceited, you hear.'

It was an unreasonable thing to say. Popo had the habit of taking a glass of rum to the pavement every morning. He never sipped the rum. But whenever he saw someone he knew he dipped his middle finger in the rum, licked it, and then waved to the man.

'We could buy rum too,' Hat used to say. 'But we don't show off like Popo.'

I myself never thought about it in that way, and one day I asked Popo about it.

Popo said, 'Boy, in the morning, when the sun shining and it still cool, and you just get up, it make you feel good to know that you could go out and stand up in the sun and have some rum.'

Popo never made any money. His wife used to go out and work, and this was easy, because they had no children. Popo said, 'Women and them like work. Man not make for work.'

Hat said, 'Popo is a man-woman. Not a proper man.'

Popo's wife had a job as a cook in a big house near my school. She used to wait for me in the afternoons and take me into the big kitchen and give me a lot of nice things to eat. The only thing I didn't like was the way she sat and watched me while I ate. It was as though I was eating for her. She asked me to call her Auntie.

She introduced me to the gardener of the big house. He was a good-looking brown man, and he loved his flowers. I liked the gardens he looked after. The flower-beds were always black and wet; and the grass green and damp and always cut. Sometimes he let me water the flower-beds. And he used to gather the cut grass into little bags which he gave me to take home to my mother. Grass was good for the hens.

One day I missed Popo's wife. She wasn't waiting for me.

Next morning I didn't see Popo dipping his finger in the glass of rum on the pavement.

And that evening I didn't see Popo's wife.

I found Popo sad in his workshop. He was sitting on a plank and twisting a bit of shaving around his fingers.

Popo said, 'Your auntie gone, boy.'

'Where, Mr Popo?'

'Ha, boy! That's the question,' and he pulled himself up there.

Popo found himself then a popular man. The news got around very quickly. And when Eddoes said one day, 'I wonder what happen to Popo. Like he got no more rum,' Hat jumped up and almost cuffed him. And then all the men began to gather in Popo's workshop, and they would talk about cricket and football and pictures – everything except women – just to try to cheer Popo up.

Popo's workshop no longer sounded with hammering and sawing. The sawdust no longer smelled fresh, and became black, almost like dirt. Popo began drinking a lot, and I didn't like him when he was drunk. He smelled of rum, and he used to cry and then grow angry and want to beat up everybody. That made him an accepted member of the gang.

Hat said, 'We was wrong about Popo. He is a man, like any of we.'

Popo liked the new companionship. He was at heart a loquacious man, and always wanted to be friendly with the men of the street and he was always surprised that he was not liked. So it looked as though he had got what he wanted. But Popo was not really happy. The friendship had come a little too late, and he found he didn't like it as much as he'd expected. Hat tried to get Popo interested in other women, but Popo wasn't interested.

Popo didn't think I was too young to be told anything.

'Boy, when you grow old as me,' he said once, 'you find that you don't care for the things you thought you woulda like if you coulda afford them.'

That was his way of talking, in riddles.

*

Then one day Popo left us.

Hat said, 'He don't have to tell me where he gone. He gone looking for he wife.'

Edward said, 'Think she going come back with he?'

Hat said, 'Let we wait and see.'

We didn't have to wait long. It came out in the papers. Hat said it was just what he expected. Popo had beaten up a man in Arima, the man had taken his wife away. It was the gardener who used to give me bags of grass.

Nothing much happened to Popo. He had to pay a fine, but they let him off otherwise. The magistrate said that Popo had better not molest his wife again.

They made a calypso about Popo that was the rage that year. It was the road-march for the Carnival, and the Andrews Sisters sang it for an American recording company:

> A certain carpenter feller went to Arima
> Looking for a mopsy called Emelda.

It was a great thing for the street.

At school, I used to say, 'The carpenter feller was a good, good friend of mine.'

And, at cricket matches, and at the races, Hat used to say, 'Know him? God, I used to drink with that man night and day. Boy, he could carry his liquor.'

*

Popo wasn't the same man when he came back to us. He growled at me when I tried to talk to him, and he drove out Hat and the others when they brought a bottle of rum to the workshop.

Hat said, 'Woman send that man mad, you hear.'

But the old noises began to be heard once more from Popo's workshop. He was working hard, and I wondered whether he was still making the thing without a name. But I was too afraid to ask.

He ran an electric light to the workshop and began working in the night-time. Vans stopped outside his house and were always depositing and taking away things. Then Popo began painting his house. He used a bright green, and he painted the roof a bright red. Hat said, 'The man really mad.'

And added, 'Like he getting married again.'

Hat wasn't too far wrong. One day, about two weeks later, Popo returned, and he brought a woman with him. It was his wife. My auntie.

'You see the sort of thing woman is,' Hat commented. 'You see the sort of thing they like. Not the man. But the new house paint up, and all the new furniture inside it. I bet you if the man in Arima had a new house and new furnitures, she wouldnta come back with Popo.'

But I didn't mind. I was glad. It was good to see Popo standing outside with his glass of rum in the mornings and dipping his finger into the rum and waving at his friends; and it was good to ask him again, 'What you making, Mr Popo?' and to get the old answer, 'Ha, boy! That's the question. I making the thing without a name.'

Popo returned very quickly to his old way of living, and he was still devoting his time to making the thing without a name. He had stopped working, and his wife got her job with the same people near my school.

People in the street were almost angry with Popo when his wife came back. They felt that all their sympathy had been mocked and wasted. And again Hat was saying, 'That blasted Popo too conceited, you hear.'

But this time Popo didn't mind.

He used to tell me, 'Boy, go home and pray tonight that you get happy like me.'

*

What happened afterwards happened so suddenly that we didn't even know it had happened. Even Hat didn't know about it until he read it in the papers. Hat always read the papers. He read them from about ten in the morning until about six in the evening.

Hat shouted out, 'But what is this I seeing?' and he showed us the headlines: CALYPSO CARPENTER JAILED

It was a fantastic story. Popo had been stealing things left and right. All the new furnitures, as Hat called them, hadn't been made by Popo. He had stolen things and simply remodelled them. He had stolen too much as a matter of fact, and had had to sell the things he didn't want. That was how he had been caught. And we understood now why the vans were always outside Popo's house. Even the paint and the brushes with which he had redecorated the house had been stolen.

Hat spoke for all of us when he said, 'That man too foolish. Why he had to sell what he thief? Just tell me that. Why?'

We agreed it was a stupid thing to do. But we felt deep inside ourselves that Popo was really a man, perhaps a bigger man than any of us.

And as for my auntie . . .

Hat said, 'How much jail he get? A year? With three months off for good behaviour, that's nine months in all. And I give she three months good behaviour too. And after that, it ain't going to have no more Emelda in Miguel Street, you hear.'

But Emelda never left Miguel Street. She not only kept her job as cook, but she started taking in washing and ironing as well. No one in the street felt sorry that Popo had gone to jail because of the shame; after all that was a thing that could happen to any of us. They felt sorry only that Emelda was going to be left alone for so long.

He came back as a hero. He was one of the boys. He was a better man than either Hat or Bogart.

But for me, he had changed. And the change made me sad.

For Popo began working.

He began making morris chairs and tables and wardrobes for people.

And when I asked him, 'Mr Popo, when you going start making the thing without a name again?' he growled at me.

'You too troublesome,' he said. 'Go away quick, before I lay my hand on you.'

3. George and The Pink House

I WAS MUCH more afraid of George than I was of Big Foot, although Big Foot was the biggest and the strongest man in the street. George was short and fat. He had a grey moustache and a big belly. He looked harmless enough but he was always muttering to himself and cursing and I never tried to become friendly with him.

He was like the donkey he had tied in the front of his yard, grey and old and silent except when it brayed loudly. You felt that George was never really in touch with what was going on around him all the time, and I found it strange that no one should have said that George was mad, while everybody said that Man-man, whom I liked, was mad.

George's house also made me feel afraid. It was a broken-down wooden building, painted pink on the outside, and the galvanized-iron roof was brown from rust. One door, the one to the right, was always left open. The inside walls had never been painted, and were grey and black with age. There was a dirty bed in one corner and in another there was a table and a stool. That was all. No curtains, no pictures on the wall. Even Bogart had a picture of Lauren Bacall in his room.

I found it hard to believe that George had a wife and a son and a daughter.

Like Popo, George was happy to let his wife do all the work in the house and the yard. They kept cows, and again I hated

George for that. Because the water from his pens made the gutters stink, and when we were playing cricket on the pavement the ball often got wet in the gutter. Boyee and Errol used to wet the ball deliberately in the stinking gutter. They wanted to make it shoot.

George's wife was never a proper person. I always thought of her just as George's wife, and that was all. And I always thought, too, that George's wife was nearly always in the cow-pen.

And while George sat on the front concrete step outside the open door of his house, his wife was busy.

George never became one of the gang in Miguel Street. He didn't seem to mind. He had his wife and his daughter and his son. He beat them all. And when the boy Elias grew too big, George beat his daughter and his wife more than ever. The blows didn't appear to do the mother any good. She just grew thinner and thinner; but the daughter, Dolly, thrived on it. She grew fatter and fatter, and giggled more and more every year. Elias, the son, grew more and more stern, but he never spoke a hard word to his father.

Hat said, 'That boy Elias have too much good mind.'

One day Bogart, of all people, said, 'Ha! I mad to break old George tail up, you hear.'

And the few times when Elias joined the crowd, Hat would say, 'Boy, I too sorry for you. Why you don't fix the old man up good?'

Elias would say, 'It is all God work.'

Elias was only fourteen or so at the time. But that was the sort of boy he was. He was serious and he had big ambitions.

I began to be terrified of George, particularly when he bought two great Alsatian dogs and tied them to pickets at the foot of the concrete steps.

Every morning and afternoon when I passed his house, he would say to the dogs, 'Shook him!'

And the dogs would bound and leap and bark; and I could see their ropes stretched tight and I always felt that the ropes would break at the next leap. Now, when Hat had an Alsatian, he made it like me. And Hat had said to me then, 'Never fraid dog. Go brave. Don't run.'

And so I used to walk slowly past George's house, lengthening out my torture.

I don't know whether George disliked me personally, or whether he simply had no use for people in general. I never discussed it with the other boys in the street, because I was too ashamed to say I was afraid of barking dogs.

Presently, though, I grew used to the dogs. And even George's laughter when I passed the house didn't worry me very much.

One day George was on the pavement as I was passing; I heard him mumbling. I heard him mumble again that afternoon and again the following day. He was saying, 'Horse-face!'

Sometimes he said, 'Like it only have horse-face people living in this place.'

Sometimes he said, 'Short-arse!'

And, 'But how it have people so short-arse in the world?'

I pretended not to hear, of course, but after a week or so I was almost in tears whenever George mumbled these things.

One evening, when we had stopped playing cricket on the pavement because Boyee had hit the ball into Miss Hilton's yard, and that was a lost ball (it counted six and out) – that evening, I asked Elias, 'but what your father have with me so? Why he does keep on calling me names?'

Hat laughed, and Elias looked a little solemn.

Hat said, 'What sort of names?'

I said, 'The fat old man does call me horse-face.' I couldn't bring myself to say the other name.

Hat began laughing.

Elias said, 'Boy, my father is a funny man. But you must forgive him. What he say don't matter. He old. He have life hard. He not educated like we here. He have a soul just like any of we, too besides.'

And he was so serious that Hat didn't laugh and whenever I walked past George's house, I kept on saying to myself, 'I must forgive him. He ain't know what he doing.'

And then Elias's mother died, and had the shabbiest and the saddest and the loneliest funeral Miguel Street had ever seen.

That empty front room became sadder and more frightening for me.

The strange thing was that I felt a little sorry for George. The Miguel Street men held a post-mortem outside Hat's house. Hat said, 'He did beat she too bad.'

Bogart nodded and drew a circle on the pavement with his right index finger.

Edward said, 'I think he kill she, you know. Boyee tell me that the evening before she dead he hear George giving the woman licks like fire.'

Hat said, 'What you think they have doctors and magistrates in this place for? For fun?'

'But I telling you,' Edward said. 'It really true. Boyee wouldn't lie about a thing like that. The woman dead from blows. I telling you. London can take it; but not George wife.'

Not one of the men said a word for George.

Boyee said something I didn't expect him to say. He said, 'The person I really feel sorry for is Dolly. You suppose he going to beat she still?'

Hat said wisely, 'Let we wait and see.'

*

Elias dropped out of our circle.

*

George was very sad for the first few days after the funeral. He drank a lot of rum and went about crying in the streets, beating his chest and asking everybody to forgive him, and to take pity on him, a poor widower.

He kept up the drinking into the following weeks, and he was still running up and down the street, making everyone feel foolish when he asked for forgiveness. 'My son Elias,' George used to say, 'my son Elias forgive me, and he is a educated boy.'

When he came to Hat, Hat said, 'What happening to your cows? You milking them? You feeding them? You want to kill your cows now too?'

George sold all his cows to Hat.

'God will say is robbery,' Hat laughed. 'I say is a bargain.'

Edward said, 'It good for George. He beginning to pay for his sins.'

'Well, I look at it this way,' Hat said. 'I give him enough money to remain drunk for two whole months.'

*

George was away from Miguel Street for a week. During that time we saw more of Dolly. She swept out the front room and begged flowers of the neighbours and put them in the room. She giggled more than ever.

Someone in the street (not me) poisoned the two Alsatians.

We hoped that George had gone away for good.

He did come back, however, still drunk, but no longer crying or helpless, and he had a woman with him. She was a very Indian woman, a little old, but she looked strong enough to handle George.

'She look like a drinker sheself,' Hat said.

This woman took control of George's house, and once more Dolly retreated into the back, where the empty cow-pens were.

We heard stories of beatings and everybody said he was sorry for Dolly and the new woman.

My heart went out to the woman and Dolly. I couldn't understand how anybody in the world would want to live with George, and I wasn't surprised when one day, about two weeks later, Popo told me, 'George new wife leave him, you ain't hear?'

Hat said, 'I wonder what he going do when the money I give him finish.'

*

We soon saw.

The pink house, almost overnight, became a full and noisy place. There were many women about, talking loudly and not paying too much attention to the way they dressed. And whenever I passed the pink house, these women shouted abusive remarks at me; and some of them did things with their mouths, inviting me to 'come to mooma'. And there were not only these new women. Many American soldiers drove up in jeeps, and Miguel Street became full of laughter and shrieks.

Hat said, 'That man George giving the street a bad name, you know.'

It was as though Miguel Street belonged to these new people. Hat and the rest of the boys were no longer assured of privacy when they sat down to talk things over on the pavement.

But Bogart became friendly with the new people and spent two or three evenings a week with them. He pretended he was disgusted at what he saw, but I didn't believe him because he was always going back.

'What happening to Dolly?' Hat asked him one day.

'She dey,' Bogart said, meaning that she was all right.

'Ah know she dey,' Hat said. 'But how she dey?'

'Well, she cleaning and cooking.'

'For everybody?'

'Everybody.'

Elias had a room of his own which he never left whenever he

came home. He ate his meals outside. He was trying to study for some important exam. He had lost interest in his family, Bogart said, or rather, implied.

George was still drinking a lot; but he was prospering. He was wearing a suit now, and a tie.

Hat said, 'He must be making a lot of money, if he have to bribe all the policemen and them.'

What I couldn't understand at all, though, was the way these new women behaved to George. They all appeared to like him as well as respect him. And George wasn't attempting to be nice in return either. He remained himself.

*

One day he said to everyone, 'Dolly ain't have no mooma now. I have to be father and mother to the child. And I say is high time Dolly get married.'

His choice fell on a man called Razor. It was hard to think of a more suitable name for this man. He was small. He was thin. He had a neat, sharp moustache above neat, tiny lips. The creases on his trousers were always sharp and clean and straight. And he was supposed to carry a knife.

Hat didn't like Dolly marrying Razor. 'He too sharp for we,' he said. 'He is the sort of man who wouldn't think anything about forgetting a knife in your back, you know.'

But Dolly still giggled.

Razor and Dolly were married at church, and they came back to a reception in the pink house. The women were all dressed up, and there were lots of American soldiers and sailors drinking and laughing and congratulating George. The women and the Americans made Dolly and Razor kiss and kiss, and they cheered. Dolly giggled.

Hat said, 'She ain't giggling, you know. She crying really.'

Elias wasn't at home that day.

The women and the Americans sang *Sweet Sixteen* and *As Time Goes By*. Then they made Dolly and Razor kiss again. Someone shouted, 'Speech!' and everybody laughed and shouted, 'Speech! Speech!'

Razor left Dolly standing by herself giggling.

'Speech! Speech!' the wedding guests called.

Dolly only giggled more.

Then George spoke out. 'Dolly, you married, it true. But don't think you too big for me to put you across my lap and cut your tail.' He said it in a jocular manner, and the guests laughed.

Then Dolly stopped giggling and looked stupidly at the people.

For a moment so brief you could scarcely measure it there was absolute silence; then an American sailor waved his hands drunkenly and shouted, 'You could put this girl to better work, George.' And everybody laughed.

Dolly picked up a handful of gravel from the yard and was making as if to throw it at the sailor. But she stopped suddenly, and burst into tears.

There was much laughing and cheering and shouting.

I never knew what happened to Dolly. Edward said one day that she was living in Sangre Grande. Hat said he saw her selling in the George Street Market. But she had left the street, left it for good. As the months went by, the women began to disappear and the numbers of jeeps that stopped outside George's house grew smaller.

'You gotta be organized,' Hat said.

Bogart nodded.

Hat added, 'And they have lots of nice places all over the place in Port of Spain these days. The trouble with George is that he too stupid for a big man.'

Hat was a prophet. Within six months, George was living alone in his pink house. I used to see him then, sitting on the steps, but he never looked at me any more. He looked old and weary and very sad.

He died soon afterwards. Hat and the boys got some money together and we buried him at Lapeyrouse Cemetery. Elias turned up for the funeral.

4. His Chosen Calling

AFTER MIDNIGHT there were two regular noises in the street. At about two o'clock you heard the sweepers; and then, just before dawn, the scavenging-carts came and you heard the men scraping off the rubbish the sweepers had gathered into heaps.

No boy in the street particularly wished to be a sweeper. But if you asked any boy what he would like to be, he would say, 'I going be a cart-driver.'

There was certainly a glamour to driving the blue carts. The men were aristocrats. They worked early in the morning, and had the rest of the day free. And then they were always going on strike. They didn't strike for much. They struck for things like a cent more a day; they struck if someone was laid off. They struck when the war began; they struck when the war ended. They struck when India got independence. They struck when Gandhi died.

Eddoes, who was a driver, was admired by most of the boys. He said his father was the best cart-driver of his day, and he told us great stories of the old man's skill. Eddoes came from a low Hindu caste, and there was a lot of truth in what he said. His skill was a sort of family skill, passing from father to son.

One day I was sweeping the pavement in front of the house where I lived, and Eddoes came and wanted to take away the broom from me. I liked sweeping and didn't want to give him the broom.

'Boy, what you know about sweeping?' Eddoes asked, laughing.

I said, 'What, it have so much to know?'

Eddoes said, 'This is my job, boy. I have experience. Wait until you big like me.'

I gave him the broom.

I was sad for a long time afterwards. It seemed that I would never never grow as big as Eddoes, never have that thing he called experience. I began to admire Eddoes more than ever; and more than ever I wanted to be a cart-driver.

But Elias was not that sort of boy.

When we who formed the Junior Miguel Street Club squatted on the pavement, talking, like Hat and Bogart and the others, about things like life and cricket and football, I said to Elias, 'So you don't want to be a cart-driver? What you want to be then? A sweeper?'

Elias spat neatly into the gutter and looked down. He said very earnestly, 'I think I going be a doctor, you hear.'

If Boyee or Errol had said something like that, we would all have laughed. But we recognized that Elias was different, that Elias had brains.

We all felt sorry for Elias. His father George brutalized the boy with blows, but Elias never cried, never spoke a word against his father.

One day I was going to Chin's shop to buy three cents' worth of butter, and I asked Elias to come with me. I didn't see George about, and I thought it was safe.

We were just about two houses away when we saw George. Elias grew scared. George came up and said sharply, 'Where you going?' And at the same time he landed a powerful cuff on Elias's jaw.

George liked beating Elias. He used to tie him with rope, and then beat him with rope he had soaked in the gutters of his cow-pen. Elias didn't cry even then. And shortly after, I would see

George laughing with Elias, and George used to say to me, 'I know what you thinking. You wondering how me and he get so friendly so quick.'

The more I disliked George, the more I liked Elias.

I was prepared to believe that he would become a doctor some day.

Errol said, 'I bet you when he come doctor and thing he go forget the rest of we. Eh, Elias?'

A small smile appeared on Elias's lips.

'Nah,' he said. 'I wouldn't be like that. I go give a lot of money and thing to you and Boyee and the rest of you fellows.' And Elias waved his small hands, and we thought we could see the Cadillac and the black bag and the tube-thing that Elias was going to have when he became a doctor.

Elias began going to the school at the other end of Miguel Street. It didn't really look like a school at all. It looked just like any house to me, but there was a sign outside that said:

TITUS HOYT, I.A. (London, External)
Passes in the Cambridge
School Certificate Guaranteed

The odd thing was that although George beat Elias at the slightest opportunity, he was very proud that his son was getting an education. 'The boy learning a hell of a lot, you know. He reading Spanish, French and Latin, and he writing Spanish, French and Latin.'

The year before his mother died, Elias sat for the Cambridge Senior School Certificate.

Titus Hoyt came down to our end of the street.

'That boy going pass with honours,' Titus Hoyt said. 'With honours.'

We saw Elias dressed in neat khaki trousers and white shirt, going to the examination room, and we looked at him with awe.

Errol said, 'Everything Elias write not remaining here, you know. Every word that boy write going to England.'

It didn't sound true.

'What you think it is at all?' Errol said. 'Elias have brains, you know.'

Elias's mother died in January, and the results came out in March.

Elias hadn't passed.

Hat looked through the list in the *Guardian* over and over again, looking for Elias's name, saying, 'You never know. People always making mistake, especially when it have so much names.'

Elias's name wasn't in the paper.

Boyee said, 'What else you expect? Who correct the papers? English man, not so? You expect them to give Elias a pass?'

Elias was with us, looking sad and not saying a word.

Hat said, 'Is a damn shame. If they know what hell the boy have to put up with, they woulda pass him quick quick.'

Titus Hoyt said, 'Don't worry. Rome wasn't built in a day. This year! This year, things going be much much better. We go show those Englishmen and them.'

Elias left us and he began living with Titus Hoyt. We saw next to nothing of him. He was working night and day.

One day in the following March, Titus Hoyt rode up to us and said, 'You hear what happen?'

'What happen?' Hat asked.

'The boy is a genius,' Titus Hoyt said.

'Which boy?' Errol asked.

'Elias.'

'What Elias do?'

'The boy gone and pass the Cambridge Senior School Certificate.'

Hat whistled. 'The Cambridge Senior School Certificate?'

Titus Hoyt smiled. 'That self. He get a third grade. His name going to be in the papers tomorrow. I always say it, and I saying it again now, this boy Elias have too much brains.'

Hat said later, 'Is too bad that Elias father dead. He was a good-for-nothing, but he wanted to see his son a educated man.'

Elias came that evening, and everybody, boys and men, gathered around him. They talked about everything but books, and Elias, too, was talking about things like pictures and girls and cricket. He was looking very solemn, too.

There was a pause once, and Hat said, 'What you going to do now, Elias? Look for work?'

Elias spat. 'Nah, I think I will write the exam again.'

I said, 'But why?'

'I want a second grade.'

We understood. He wanted to be a doctor.

Elias sat down on the pavement, and said, 'Yes, boy. I think I going to take that exam again, and this year I going to be so good that this Mr Cambridge go bawl when he read what I write for him.'

We were silent, in wonder.

'Is the English and litritcher that does beat me.'

In Elias's mouth litritcher was the most beautiful word I heard. It sounded like something to eat, something rich like chocolate.

Hat said, 'You mean you have to read a lot of poultry and thing?'

Elias nodded. We felt it wasn't fair, making a boy like Elias do litritcher and poultry.

*

Elias moved back into the pink house which had been empty since his father died. He was studying and working. He went back to

Titus Hoyt's school, not as pupil, but as a teacher, and Titus Hoyt said he was giving him forty dollars a month.

Titus Hoyt added, 'He worth it, too. He is one of the brightest boys in Port of Spain.'

Now that Elias was back with us, we noticed him better. He was the cleanest boy in the street. He bathed twice a day and scrubbed his teeth twice a day. He did all this standing up at the tap in front of the house. He swept the house every morning before going to school. He was the opposite of his father. His father was short and fat and dirty. He was tall and thin and clean. His father drank and swore. He never drank and no one ever heard him use a bad word.

My mother used to say to me, 'Why you don't take after Elias? I really don't know what sort of son God give me, you hear.'

And whenever Hat or Edward beat Boyee and Errol, they always said, 'Why you beating we for? Not everybody could be like Elias, you know.'

Hat used to say, 'And it ain't only that he got brains. The boy Elias have nice *ways* too.'

So I think I was a little glad when Elias sat the examination for the third time, and failed.

Hat said, 'You see how we catch these Englishmen and them. Nobody here can tell me that the boy didn't pass the exam, but you think they go want to give him a better grade? Ha!'

And everybody said, 'Is a real shame.'

And when Hat asked Elias, 'What you going to do now, boy?' Elias said, 'You know, I think I go take up a job. I think I go be a sanitary inspector.'

We saw him in khaki uniform and khaki topee, going from house to house with a little note-book.

'Yes,' Elias said. 'Sanitary inspector, that's what I going to be.'

Hat said, 'It have a lot of money in that, I think. I hear your father George uses to pay the sanitary inspector five dollars a month to keep his mouth shut. Let we say you get about ten or even eight people like that. That's – let me see . . . ten fives is fifty, eight fives is forty. There, fifty, forty dollars straight. And mark you, that ain't counting your salary.'

Elias said, 'Is not the money I thinking about. I really like the work.'

It was easy to understand that.

Elias said, 'But it have a exam, you know.'

Hat said, 'But they don't send the papers to England for that?'

Elias said, 'Nah, but still, I fraid exams and things, you know. I ain't have any luck with them.'

Boyee said, 'But I thought you was thinking of taking up doctoring.'

Hat said, 'Boyee, I going to cut your little tail if you don't shut up.'

But Boyee didn't mean anything bad.

Elias said, 'I change my mind. I think I want to be a sanitary inspector. I really like the work.'

*

For three years Elias sat the sanitary inspectors' examination, and he failed every time.

Elias began saying, 'But what the hell you expect in Trinidad? You got to bribe everybody if you want to get your toenail cut.'

Hat said, 'I meet a man from a boat the other day, and he tell me that the sanitary inspector exams in British Guiana much easier. You could go to B.G. and take the exams there and come back and work here.'

Elias flew to B.G., wrote the exam, failed it, and flew back.

Hat said, 'I meet a man from Barbados. He tell me that the exams easier in Barbados. It easy, easy, he say.'

Elias flew to Barbados, wrote the exam, failed it, and flew back.

Hat said, 'I meet a man from Grenada the other day – '

Elias said, 'Shut your arse up, before it have trouble between we in this street.'

*

A few years later I sat the Cambridge Senior School Certificate Examination myself, and Mr Cambridge gave me a second grade. I applied for a job in the Customs, and it didn't cost me much to get it. I got a khaki uniform with brass buttons, and a cap. Very much like the sanitary inspector's uniform.

Elias wanted to beat me up the first day I wore the uniform.

'What your mother do to get you that?' he shouted, and I was going for him, when Eddoes put a stop to it.

Eddoes said, 'He just sad and jealous. He don't mean anything.'

For Elias had become one of the street aristocrats. He was driving the scavenging-carts.

'No theory here,' Elias used to say. 'This is the practical. I really like the work.'

5. Man-man

EVERYBODY IN Miguel Street said that Man-man was mad, and so they left him alone. But I am not so sure now that he was mad, and I can think of many people much madder than Man-man ever was.

He didn't look mad. He was a man of medium height, thin; and he wasn't bad-looking either. He never stared at you the way I expected a mad man to do; and when you spoke to him you were sure of getting a very reasonable reply.

But he did have some curious habits.

He went up for every election, city council or legislative council, and then he stuck posters everywhere in the district. These posters were well printed. They just had the word 'Vote' and below that, Man-man's picture.

At every election he got exactly three votes. That I couldn't understand. Man-man voted for himself, but who were the other two?

I asked Hat.

Hat said, 'I really can't say, boy. Is a real mystery. Perhaps is two jokers. But they is funny sort of jokers if they do the same thing so many times. They must be mad just like he.'

And for a long time the thought of these two mad men who voted for Man-man haunted me. Every time I saw someone doing anything just a little bit odd, I wondered, 'Is he who vote for Man-man?'

At large in the city were these two men of mystery.

Man-man never worked. But he was never idle. He was hypnotized by the word, particularly the written word, and he would spend a whole day writing a single word.

One day I met Man-man at the corner of Miguel Street.

'Boy, where you going?' Man-man asked.

'I going to school,' I said.

And Man-man, looking at me solemnly, said in a mocking way, 'So you goes to school, eh?'

I said automatically, 'Yes, I goes to school.' And I found that without intending it I had imitated Man-man's correct and very English accent.

That again was another mystery about Man-man. His accent. If you shut your eyes while he spoke, you would believe an Englishman – a good-class Englishman who wasn't particular about grammar – was talking to you.

Man-man said, as though speaking to himself, 'So the little man is going to school.'

Then he forgot me, and took out a long stick of chalk from his pocket and began writing on the pavement. He drew a very big S in outline and then filled it in, and then the C and the H and the O. But then he started making several O's, each smaller than the last, until he was writing in cursive, O after flowing O.

When I came home for lunch, he had got to French Street, and he was still writing O's, rubbing off mistakes with a rag.

In the afternoon he had gone round the block and was practically back in Miguel Street.

I went home, changed from my school-clothes into my home-clothes and went out to the street.

He was now half-way up Miguel Street.

He said, 'So the little man gone to school today?'

I said, 'Yes.'

He stood up and straightened his back.

Then he squatted again and drew the outline of a Massive L and filled that in slowly and lovingly.

When it was finished, he stood up and said, 'You finish your work. I finish mine.'

Or it was like this. If you told Man-man you were going to the cricket, he would write CRICK and then concentrate on the E's until he saw you again.

One day Man-man went to the big café at the top of Miguel Street and began barking and growling at the customers on the stools as though he were a dog. The owner, a big Portuguese man with hairy hands, said, 'Man-man, get out of this shop before I tangle with you.'

Man-man just laughed.

They threw Man-man out.

Next day, the owner found that someone had entered his café during the night, and had left all the doors open. But nothing was missing.

Hat said, 'One thing you must never do is trouble Man-man. He remember everything.'

That night the café was entered again and the doors again left open.

The following night the café was entered and this time little blobs of excrement were left on the centre of every stool and on top of every table and at regular intervals along the counter.

The owner of the café was the laughing-stock of the street for several weeks, and it was only after a long time that people began going to the café again.

Hat said, 'Is just like I say. Boy, I don't like meddling with that man. These people really bad-mind, you know. God make them that way.'

It was things like this that made people leave Man-man alone. The only friend he had was a little mongrel dog, white with black spots on the ears. The dog was like Man-man in a way, too. It was a curious dog. It never barked, never looked at you, and if you looked at it, it looked away. It never made friends with any other dog, and if some dog tried either to get friendly or aggressive, Man-man's dog gave it a brief look of disdain and ambled away, without looking back.

Man-man loved his dog, and the dog loved Man-man. They were made for each other, and Man-man couldn't have made a living without his dog.

Man-man appeared to exercise a great control over the movements of his dog's bowels.

Hat said, 'That does really beat me. I can't make that one out.'

It all began in Miguel Street.

One morning, several women got up to find that the clothes they had left to bleach overnight had been sullied by the droppings of a dog. No one wanted to use the sheets and the shirts after that, and when Man-man called, everyone was willing to give him the dirty clothes.

Man-man used to sell these clothes.

Hat said, 'Is things like this that make me wonder whether the man really mad.'

From Miguel Street Man-man's activities spread, and all the people who had suffered from Man-man's dog were anxious to get other people to suffer the same thing.

We in Miguel Street became a little proud of him.

*

I don't know what it was that caused Man-man to turn good. Perhaps the death of his dog had something to do with it. The dog was run over by a car, and it gave, Hat said, just one short squeak, and then it was silent.

Man-man wandered about for days, looking dazed and lost.

He no longer wrote words on the pavement; no longer spoke

to me or to any of the other boys in the street. He began talking to himself, clasping his hands and shaking as though he had ague.

Then one day he said he had seen God after having a bath.

This didn't surprise many of us. Seeing God was quite common in Port of Spain, and, indeed, in Trinidad at that time. Ganesh Pundit, the mystic masseur from Fuente Grove, had started it. He had seen God, too, and had published a little booklet called *What God Told Me*. Many rival mystics and not a few masseurs had announced the same thing, and I suppose it was natural that since God was in the area Man-man should see Him.

Man-man began preaching at the corner of Miguel Street, under the awning of Mary's shop. He did this every Saturday night. He let his beard grow and he dressed in a long white robe. He got a Bible and other holy things and stood in the white light of an acetylene lamp and preached. He was an impressive preacher, and he preached in an odd way. He made women cry, and he made people like Hat really worried.

He used to hold the Bible in his right hand and slap it with his left and say in his perfect English accent, 'I have been talking to God these few days, and what he tell me about you people wasn't really nice to hear. These days you hear all the politicians and them talking about making the island self-sufficient. You know what God tell me last night? Last night self, just after I finish eating? God say, "Man-man, come and have a look at these people." He show me husband eating wife and wife eating husband. He show me father eating son and mother eating daughter. He show me brother eating sister and sister eating brother. That is what these politicians and them mean by saying that the island going to become self-sufficient. But, brethren, it not too late now to turn to God.'

*

I used to get nightmares every Saturday night after hearing Man-man preach. But the odd thing was that the more he frightened people the more they came to hear him preach. And when the collection was made they gave him more than ever.

In the week-days he just walked about, in his white robe, and he begged for food. He said he had done what Jesus ordered and he had given away all his goods. With his long black beard and his bright deep eyes, you couldn't refuse him anything. He noticed me no longer, and never asked me, 'So you goes to school?'

The people in Miguel Street didn't know what to make of the change. They tried to comfort themselves by saying that Man-man was really mad, but, like me, I think they weren't sure that Man-man wasn't really right.

What happened afterwards wasn't really unexpected.

Man-man announced that he was a new Messiah.

Hat said one day, 'You ain't hear the latest?'

We said, 'What?'

'Is about Man-man. He say he going to be crucified one of these days.'

'Nobody go touch him,' Edward said. 'Everybody fraid of him now.'

Hat explained. 'Not, it ain't that. He going to crucify hisself. One of these Fridays he going to Blue Basin and tie hisself to a cross and let people stone him.'

Somebody – Errol, I think – laughed, but finding that no one laughed with him, fell silent again.

But on top of our wonder and worry, we had this great pride in knowing that Man-man came from Miguel Street.

Little hand-written notices began appearing in the shops and cafés and on the gates of some houses, announcing Man-man's forthcoming crucifixion.

'They going to have a big crowd in Blue Basin,' Hat announced, and added with pride, 'and I hear they sending some police too.'

That day, early in the morning, before the shops opened and the trolley-buses began running in Ariapita Avenue, the big crowd assembled at the corner of Miguel Street. There were lots of men dressed in black and even more women dressed in white. They were singing hymns. There were also about twenty policemen, but they were not singing hymns.

When Man-man appeared, looking very thin and very holy, women cried and rushed to touch his gown. The police stood by, prepared to handle anything.

A van came with a great wooden cross.

Hat, looking unhappy in his serge suit, said, 'They tell me it make from match-wood. It ain't heavy. It light light.'

Edward said, in a snapping sort of way, 'That matter? Is the heart and the spirit that matter.'

Hat said, 'I ain't saying nothing.'

Some men began taking the cross from the van to give it to Man-man, but he stopped them. His English accent sounded impressive in the early morning. 'Not here. Leave it for Blue Basin.'

Hat was disappointed.

We walked to Blue Basin, the waterfall in the mountains to the north-west of Port of Spain, and we got there in two hours. Man-man began carrying the cross from the road, up the rocky path and then down to the Basin.

Some men put up the cross, and tied Man-man to it.

Man-man said, 'Stone me, brethren.'

The women wept and flung bits of sand and gravel at his feet.

Man-man groaned and said, 'Father, forgive them. They ain't know what they doing.' Then he screamed out, 'Stone me, brethren!'

A pebble the size of an egg struck him on the chest.

Man-man cried, 'Stone, stone, STONE me, brethren! I forgive you.'

Edward said, 'The man really brave.'

People began flinging really big stones at Man-man, aiming at his face and chest.

Man-man looked hurt and surprised. He shouted, 'What the hell is this? What the hell you people think you doing? Look, get me down from this thing quick, let me down quick, and I go settle with that son of a bitch who pelt a stone at me.'

From where Edward and Hat and the rest of us stood, it sounded like a cry of agony.

A bigger stone struck Man-man; the women flung the sand and gravel at him.

We heard Man-man's shout, clear and loud, 'Cut this stupidness out. Cut it out, I tell you. I finish with this arseness, you hear.' And then he began cursing so loudly and coarsely that the people stopped in surprise.

The police took away Man-man.

The authorities kept him for observation. Then for good.

6. B. Wordsworth

THREE BEGGARS CALLED punctually every day at the hospitable houses in Miguel Street. At about ten an Indian came in his dhoti and white jacket, and we poured a tin of rice into the sack he carried on his back. At twelve an old woman smoking a clay pipe came and she got a cent. At two a blind man led by a boy called for his penny.

Sometimes we had a rogue. One day a man called and said he was hungry. We gave him a meal. He asked for a cigarette and wouldn't go until we had lit it for him. That man never came again.

The strangest caller came one afternoon at about four o'clock. I had come back from school and was in my home-clothes. The man said to me, 'Sonny, may I come inside your yard?'

He was a small man and he was tidily dressed. He wore a hat, a white shirt and black trousers.

I asked, 'What you want?'

He said, 'I want to watch your bees.'

We had four small gru-gru palm trees and they were full of uninvited bees.

I ran up the steps and shouted, 'Ma, it have a man outside here. He say he want to watch the bees.'

My mother came out, looked at the man and asked in an unfriendly way, 'What you want?'

The man said, 'I want to watch your bees.'

His English was so good, it didn't sound natural, and I could see my mother was worried.

She said to me, 'Stay here and watch him while he watch the bees.'

The man said, 'Thank you, Madam. You have done a good deed today.'

He spoke very slowly and very correctly as though every word was costing him money.

We watched the bees, this man and I, for about an hour, squatting near the palm trees.

The man said, 'I like watching bees. Sonny, do you like watching bees?'

I said, 'I ain't have the time.'

He shook his head sadly. He said, 'That's what I do, I just watch. I can watch ants for days. Have you ever watched ants? And scorpions, and centipedes, and *congorees* – have you watched those?'

I shook my head.

I said, 'What you does do, mister?'

He got up and said, 'I am a poet.'

I said, 'A good poet?'

He said, 'The greatest in the world.'

'What your name, mister?'

'B. Wordsworth.'

'B for Bill?'

'Black. Black Wordsworth. White Wordsworth was my brother. We share one heart. I can watch a small flower like the morning glory and cry.'

I said, 'Why you does cry?'

'Why, boy? Why? You will know when you grow up. You're a poet, too, you know. And when you're a poet you can cry for everything.'

I couldn't laugh.

He said, 'You like your mother?'

'When she not beating me.'

He pulled out a printed sheet from his hip-pocket and said, 'On this paper is the greatest poem about mothers and I'm going to sell it to you at a bargain price. For four cents.'

I went inside and I said, 'Ma, you want to buy a poetry for four cents?'

My mother said, 'Tell that blasted man to haul his tail away from my yard, you hear.'

I said to B. Wordsworth, 'My mother say she ain't have four cents.'

B. Wordsworth said, 'It is the poet's tragedy.'

And he put the paper back in his pocket. He didn't seem to mind.

I said, 'Is a funny way to go round selling poetry like that. Only calypsonians do that sort of thing. A lot of people does buy?'

He said, 'No one has yet bought a single copy.'

'But why you does keep on going round, then?'

He said, 'In this way I watch many things, and I always hope to meet poets.'

I said, 'You really think I is a poet?'

'You're as good as me,' he said.

And when B. Wordsworth left, I prayed I would see him again.

*

About a week later, coming back from school one afternoon, I met him at the corner of Miguel Street.

He said, 'I have been waiting for you for a long time.'

I said, 'You sell any poetry yet?'

He shook his head.

He said, 'In my yard I have the best mango tree in Port of Spain. And now the mangoes are ripe and red and very sweet and juicy. I have waited here for you to tell you this and to invite you to come and eat some of my mangoes.'

He lived in Alberto Street in a one-roomed hut placed right in the centre of the lot. The yard seemed all green. There was the big mango tree. There was a coconut tree and there was a plum tree. The place looked wild, as though it wasn't in the city at all. You couldn't see all the big concrete houses in the street.

He was right. The mangoes were sweet and juicy. I ate about six, and the yellow mango juice ran down my arms to my elbows and down my mouth to my chin and my shirt was stained.

My mother said when I got home, 'Where you was? You think you is a man now and could go all over the place? Go cut a whip for me.'

She beat me rather badly, and I ran out of the house swearing that I would never come back. I went to B. Wordsworth's house. I was so angry, my nose was bleeding.

B. Wordsworth said, 'Stop crying, and we will go for a walk.'

I stopped crying, but I was breathing short. We went for a walk. We walked down St Clair Avenue to the Savannah and we walked to the race-course.

B. Wordsworth said, 'Now, let us lie on the grass and look up at the sky, and I want you to think how far those stars are from us.'

*

I did as he told me, and I saw what he meant. I felt like nothing, and at the same time I had never felt so big and great in all my life. I forgot all my anger and all my tears and all the blows.

When I said I was better, he began telling me the names of the stars, and I particularly remembered the constellation of Orion the Hunter, though I don't really know why. I can spot Orion even today, but I have forgotten the rest.

Then a light was flashed into our faces, and we saw a policeman. We got up from the grass.

The policeman said, 'What you doing here?'

B. Wordsworth said, 'I have been asking myself the same question for forty years.'

We became friends, B. Wordsworth and I. He told me, 'You must never tell anybody about me and about the mango tree and the coconut tree and the plum tree. You must keep that a secret. If you tell anybody, I will know, because I am a poet.'

I gave him my word and I kept it.

I liked his little room. It had no more furniture than George's front room, but it looked cleaner and healthier. But it also looked lonely.

One day I asked him, 'Mister Wordsworth, why you does keep all this bush in your yard? Ain't it does make the place damp?'

He said, 'Listen, and I will tell you a story. Once upon a time a boy and girl met each other and they fell in love. They loved each other so much they got married. They were both poets. He loved words. She loved grass and flowers and trees. They lived happily in a single room, and then one day, the girl poet said to the boy poet, "We are going to have another poet in the family." But this poet was never born, because the girl died, and the young poet died with her, inside her. And the girl's husband was very sad, and he said he would never touch a thing in the girl's garden. And so the garden remained, and grew high and wild.'

I looked at B. Wordsworth, and as he told me this lovely story, he seemed to grow older. I understood his story.

We went for long walks together. We went to the Botanical Gardens and the Rock Gardens. We climbed Chancellor Hill in the late afternoon and watched the darkness fall on Port of Spain, and watched the lights go on in the city and on the ships in the harbour.

He did everything as though he were doing it for the first time in his life. He did everything as though he were doing some church rite.

He would say to me, 'Now, how about having some ice-cream?'

And when I said, yes, he would grow very serious and say, 'Now, which café shall we patronize?' As though it were a very important thing. He would think for some time about it, and finally say, 'I think I will go and negotiate the purchase with that shop.'

The world became a most exciting place.

*

One day, when I was in his yard, he said to me, 'I have a great secret which I am now going to tell you.'

I said, 'It really secret?'

'At the moment, yes.'

I looked at him, and he looked at me. He said, 'This is just between you and me, remember. I am writing a poem.'

'Oh.' I was disappointed.

He said, 'But this is a different sort of poem. This is the greatest poem in the world.'

I whistled.

He said, 'I have been working on it for more than five years now. I will finish it in about twenty-two years from now, that is, if I keep on writing at the present rate.'

'You does write a lot, then?'

He said, 'Not any more. I just write one line a month. But I make sure it is a good line.'

I asked, 'What was last month's good line?'

He looked up at the sky, and said, '*The past is deep.*'

I said, 'It is a beautiful line.'

B. Wordsworth said, 'I hope to distil the experiences of a whole month into that single line of poetry. So, in twenty-two years, I shall have written a poem that will sing to all humanity.'

I was filled with wonder.

*

Our walks continued. We walked along the sea-wall at Docksite one day, and I said, 'Mr Wordsworth, if I drop this pin in the water, you think it will float?'

He said, 'This is a strange world. Drop your pin, and let us see what will happen.'

The pin sank.

I said, 'How is the poem this month?'

But he never told me any other line. He merely said, 'Oh, it comes, you know. It comes.'

Or we would sit on the sea-wall and watch the liners come into the harbour.

But of the greatest poem in the world I heard no more.

*

I felt he was growing older.

*

'How you does live, Mr Wordsworth?' I asked him one day.

He said, 'You mean how I get money?'

When I nodded, he laughed in a crooked way.

He said, 'I sing calypsoes in the calypso season.'

'And that last you the rest of the year?'

'It is enough.'

'But you will be the richest man in the world when you write the greatest poem?'

He didn't reply.

*

One day when I went to see him in his little house, I found him lying on his little bed. He looked so old and so weak, that I found myself wanting to cry.

He said, 'The poem is not going well.'

He wasn't looking at me. He was looking through the window at the coconut tree, and he was speaking as though I wasn't there. He said, 'When I was twenty I felt the power within myself.' Then, almost in front of my eyes, I could see his face growing older and more tired. He said, 'But that – that was a long time ago.'

And then – I felt it so keenly, it was as though I had been slapped by my mother. I could see it clearly on his face. It was there for everyone to see. Death on the shrinking face.

He looked at me, and saw my tears and sat up.

He said, 'Come.' I went and sat on his knees.

He looked into my eyes, and he said, 'Oh, you can see it, too. I always knew you had the poet's eye.'

He didn't even look sad, and that made me burst out crying loudly.

He pulled me to his thin chest, and said, 'Do you want me to tell you a funny story?' and he smiled encouragingly at me.

But I couldn't reply.

He said, 'When I have finished this story, I want you to promise that you will go away and never come back to see me. Do you promise?'

I nodded.

He said, 'Good. Well, listen. That story I told you about the boy poet and the girl poet, do you remember that? That wasn't true. It was something I just made up. All this talk about poetry and the greatest poem in the world, that wasn't true, either. Isn't that the funniest thing you have heard?'

But his voice broke.

I left the house, and ran home crying, like a poet, for everything I saw.

*

I walked along Alberto Street a year later, but I could find no sign of the poet's house. It hadn't vanished, just like that. It had been pulled down, and a big, two-storeyed building had taken its place. The mango tree and the plum tree and the coconut tree had all been cut down, and there was brick and concrete everywhere.

It was just as though B. Wordsworth had never existed.

7. The Coward

BIG FOOT WAS really big and really black, and everybody in Miguel Street was afraid of him. It wasn't his bigness or his blackness that people feared, for there were blacker and bigger people about. People were afraid of him because he was so silent and sulky; he *looked* dangerous, like those terrible dogs that never bark but just look at you from the corner of their eyes.

Hat used to say, 'Is only a form of showing off, you know, all this quietness he does give us. He quiet just because he ain't have anything to say, that's all.'

Yet you could hear Hat telling all sorts of people at the races and cricket, 'Big Foot and me? We is bosom pals, man. We grow up together.'

And at school I myself used to say, 'Big Foot does live in my street, you hear. I know him good good, and if any one of all you touch me, I go tell Big Foot.'

At that time I had never spoken a single word to Big Foot.

We in Miguel Street were proud to claim him because he was something of a character in Port of Spain, and had quite a reputation. It was Big Foot who flung the stone at Radio Trinidad building one day and broke a window. When the magistrate asked why he did it, Big Foot just said, 'To wake them up.'

A well-wisher paid the fine for him.

Then there was the time he got a job driving one of the diesel-buses. He drove the bus out of the city to Carenage, five miles

[50]

away, and told the passengers to get out and bathe. He stood by to see that they did.

After that he got a job as a postman, and he had a great time misplacing people's letters. They found him at Docksite, with the bag half full of letters, soaking his big feet in the Gulf of Paria.

He said, 'Is hard work, walking all over the place, delivering people letters. You come like a postage stamp, man.'

All Trinidad thought of him as a comedian, but we who knew him thought otherwise.

It was people like Big Foot who gave the steel-bands a bad name. Big Foot was always ready to start a fight with another band, but he looked so big and dangerous that he himself was never involved in any fight, and he never went to jail for more than three months or so at a time.

Hat, especially, was afraid of Big Foot. Hat often said, 'I don't know why they don't lose Big Foot in jail, you know.'

You would have thought that when he was beating his pans and dancing in the street at Carnival, Big Foot would at least smile and look happy. But no. It was on occasions like this that he prepared his sulkiest and grimmest face; and when you saw him beating a pan, you felt, to judge by his earnestness, that he was doing some sacred act.

One day a big crowd of us — Hat, Edward, Eddoes, Boyee, Errol and myself — went to the cinema. We were sitting in a row, laughing and talking all during the film, having a good time.

A voice from behind said, very quietly, 'Shut up.'

We turned and saw Big Foot.

He lazily pulled out a knife from his trouser pocket, flicked the blade open, and stuck it in the back of my chair.

He looked up at the screen and said in a frightening friendly way, 'Talk.'

We didn't say a word for the rest of the film.

Afterwards Hat said, 'You does only get policeman son behaving in that way. Policeman son and priest son.'

Boyee said, 'You mean Big Foot is priest son?'

Hat said, 'You too stupid. Priests and them does have children?'

We heard a lot about Big Foot's father from Hat. It seemed he was as much a terror as Big Foot. Sometimes when Boyee and Errol and I were comparing notes about beatings, Boyee said, 'The blows we get is nothing to what Big Foot uses to get from his father. That is how he get so big, you know. I meet a boy from Belmont the other day in the Savannah, and this boy tell me that blows does make you grow.'

Errol said, 'You is a blasted fool, man. How you does let people give you stupidness like that?'

Once Hat said, 'Every day Big Foot father, the policeman, giving Big Foot blows. Like medicine. Three times a day after meals. And hear Big Foot talk afterwards. He used to say, "When I get big and have children, I go beat them, beat them."'

I didn't say it then, because I was ashamed; but I had often felt the same way when my mother beat me.

I asked Hat, 'And Big Foot mother? She used to beat him too?'

Hat said, 'Oh, God! That woulda kill him. Big Foot didn't have any mother. His father didn't married, thank God.'

*

The Americans were crawling all over Port of Spain in those days, making the city really hot. Children didn't take long to find out that they were easy people, always ready to give with both hands. Hat began working a small racket. He had five of us going all over the district begging for chewing gum and chocolate. For every packet of chewing gum we gave him we got a cent. Sometimes I made as much as twelve cents in a day. Some boy told me later that Hat was selling the chewing gum for six cents a packet, but I didn't believe it.

One afternoon, standing on the pavement outside my house, I saw an American soldier down the street, coming towards me. It was about two o'clock in the afternoon, very hot, and the street was practically empty.

The American behaved in a very surprising way when I sprinted down to ask, 'Got any gum, Joe?'

He mumbled something about begging kids and I think he was going to slap me or cuff me. He wasn't very big, but I was afraid. I think he was drunk.

He set his mouth.

A gruff voice said, 'Look, leave the boy alone, you hear.'

It was Big Foot.

Not another word was said. The American, suddenly humble, walked away, making a great pretence of not being in a hurry.

Big Foot didn't even look at me.

I never said again, 'Got any gum, Joe?'

*

Yet this did not make me like Big Foot. I was, I believe, a little more afraid of him.

I told Hat about the American and Big Foot.

Hat said, 'All the Americans not like that. You can't throw away twelve cents a day like that.'

But I refused to beg any more.

I said, 'If it wasn't for Big Foot, the man woulda kill me.'

Hat said, 'You know, is a good thing Big Foot father dead before Big Foot really get big.'

I said, 'What happen to Big Foot father, then?'

Hat said, 'You ain't hear? It was a famous thing. A crowd of black people beat him up and kill him in 1937 when they was having the riots in the oilfields. Big Foot father was playing hero, just like Big Foot playing hero now.'

I said, 'Hat, why you don't like Big Foot?'

Hat said, 'I ain't have anything against him.'

I said, 'Why you fraid him so, then?'

Hat said, 'Ain't you fraid him too?'

I nodded. 'But I feel you do him something and you worried.'

Hat said, 'Nothing really. It just funny. The rest of we use to give Big Foot hell too. He was thin thin when he was small, you know, and we use to have a helluva time chasing him all over the place. He couldn't run at all.'

I felt sorry for Big Foot.

I said, 'How that funny?'

Hat said, 'You go hear. You know the upshot? Big Foot come the best runner out of all of we. In the school sports he run the hundred yards in ten point four seconds. That is what they say, but you know how Trinidad people can't count time. Anyway, then we all want to come friendly with him. But he don't want we at all at all.'

And I wondered then why Big Foot held himself back from beating Hat and the rest of the people who had bullied him when he was a boy.

But still I didn't like him.

*

Big Foot became a carpenter for a while, and actually built two or three enormous wardrobes, rough, ugly things. But he sold them. And then he became a mason. There is no stupid pride among Trinidad craftsmen. No one is a specialist.

He came to our yard one day to do a job.

I stood by and watched him. I didn't speak to him, and he didn't speak to me. I noticed that he used his feet as a trowel. He mumbled, 'Is hard work, bending down all the time.'

He did the job well enough. His feet were not big for nothing.

About four o'clock he knocked off, and spoke to me.

He said, 'Boy, let we go for a walk. I hot and I want to cool off.'

I didn't want to go, but I felt I had to.

We went to the sea-wall at Docksite and watched the sea. Soon it began to grow dark. The lights came on in the harbour. The world seemed very big, dark, and silent. We stood up without speaking a word.

Then a sudden sharp yap very near us tore the silence.

The suddenness and strangeness of the noise paralysed me for a moment.

It was only a dog; a small white and black dog with large flapping ears. It was dripping wet, and was wagging its tail out of pure friendliness.

I said, 'Come, boy,' and the dog shook off the water from its coat on me and then jumped all over me, yapping and squirming.

I had forgotten Big Foot, and when I looked for him I saw him about twenty yards away running for all he was worth.

I shouted, 'Is all right, Big Foot.'

But he stopped before he heard my shout.

He cried out loudly, 'Oh God, I dead, I dead. A big big bottle cut up my foot.'

I and the dog ran to him.

But when the dog came to him he seemed to forget his foot which was bleeding badly. He began hugging and stroking the wet dog, and laughing in a crazy way.

*

He had cut his foot very badly, and next day I saw it wrapped up. He couldn't come to finish the work he had begun in our yard.

I felt I knew more about Big Foot than any man in Miguel Street, and I was afraid that I knew so much. I felt like one of those small men in gangster films who know too much and get killed.

And thereafter I was always conscious that Big Foot knew what I was thinking. I felt his fear that I would tell.

But although I was bursting with Big Foot's secret I told no one. I would have liked to reassure him but there was no means.

His presence in the street became something that haunted me. And it was all I could do to stop myself telling Hat, 'I not fraid of Big Foot. I don't know why you fraid him so.'

*

Errol, Boyee, and myself sat on the pavement discussing the war.

Errol said, 'If they just make Lord Anthony Eden Prime Minister, we go beat up the Germans and them bad bad.'

Boyee said, 'What Lord Eden go do so?'

Errol just haaed, in a very knowing way.

I said, 'Yes, I always think that if they make Lord Anthony Eden Prime Minister, the war go end quick quick.'

Boyee said, 'You people just don't know the Germans. The Germans strong like hell, you know. A boy was telling me that these Germans and them could eat a nail with their teeth alone.'

Errol said, 'But we have Americans on we side now.'

Boyee said, 'But they not big like the Germans. All the Germans and them big big and strong like Big Foot, you know, and they braver than Big Foot.'

Errol, said, 'Shh! Look, he coming.'

Big Foot was very near, and I felt he could hear the conversation. He was looking at me, and there was a curious look in his eyes.

Boyee said, 'Why you shhhing me so for? I ain't saying anything bad. I just saying that the Germans brave as Big Foot.'

Just for a moment, I saw the begging look in Big Foot's eyes. I looked away.

When Big Foot had passed, Errol said to me, 'Like Big Foot have something with you, boy.'

*

One afternoon Hat was reading the morning paper. He shouted to us, 'But look at what I reading here, man.'

We asked, 'What happening now?'

Hat said, 'Is about Big Foot.'

Boyee said, 'What, they throw him in jail again?'

Hat said, 'Big Foot taking up boxing.'

I understood more than I could say.

Hat said, 'He go get his tail mash up. If he think that boxing is just throwing yourself around, he go find out his mistake.'

The newspapers made a big thing out of it. The most popular headline was *Prankster Turns Pugilist*.

And when I next saw Big Foot, I felt I could look him in the eyes.

And now I wasn't afraid of him, I was afraid for him.

But I had no need. Big Foot had what the sports-writers all called a 'phenomenal success'. He knocked out fighter after fighter, and Miguel Street grew more afraid of him and more proud of him.

Hat said, 'Is only because he only fighting stupid little people. He ain't meet anybody yet that have real class.'

Big Foot seemed to have forgotten me. His eyes no longer sought mine whenever we met, and he no longer stopped to talk to me.

He was the terror of the street. I, like everybody else, was frightened of him. As before, I preferred it that way.

He even began showing off more.

We used to see him running up and down Miguel Street in stupid-looking maroon shorts and he resolutely refused to notice anybody.

Hat was terrified.

He said, 'They shouldn't let a man who go to jail box.'

*

An Englishman came to Trinidad one day and the papers ran to interview him. The man said he was a boxer and a champion of the Royal Air Force. Next morning his picture appeared.

Two days later another picture of him appeared. This time he was dressed only in black shorts, and he had squared up towards the cameraman with his boxing gloves on.

The headline said, '*Who will fight this man?*'

And Trinidad answered, 'Big Foot will fight this man.'

The excitement was intense when Big Foot agreed. Miguel Street was in the news, and even Hat was pleased.

Hat said, 'I know is stupid to say, but I hope Big Foot beat him.' And he went around the district placing bets with everyone who had money to throw away.

We turned up in strength at the stadium on the night.

Hat rushed madly here and there, waving a twenty-dollar bill, shouting, 'Twenty to five, Big Foot beat him.'

I bet Boyee six cents that Big Foot would lose.

And, in truth, when Big Foot came out to the ring, dancing disdainfully in the ring, without looking at anybody in the crowd, we felt pleased.

Hat shouted, 'That is man!'

I couldn't bear to look at the fight. I looked all the time at the only woman in the crowd. She was an American or a Canadian woman and she was nibbling at peanuts. She was so blonde, her hair looked like straw. Whenever a blow was landed, the crowd roared, and the woman pulled in her lips as though she had given the blow, and then she nibbled furiously at her peanuts. She never shouted or got up or waved her hands. I hated that woman.

The roars grew louder and more frequent.

I could hear Hat shouting, 'Come on, Big Foot. Beat him up.

Beat him up, man.' Then, with panic in his voice, 'Remember your father.'

But Hat's shouts died away.

Big Foot had lost the fight, on points.

Hat paid out about a hundred dollars in five minutes.

He said, 'I go have to sell the brown and white cow, the one I buy from George.'

Edward said, 'Is God work.'

Boyee said to me, 'I go give you your six cents tomorrow.'

I said, 'Six cents *tomorrow*? But what you think I is? A millionaire? Look, man, give me money now now, you hear.'

He paid up.

But the crowd was laughing, laughing.

I looked at the ring.

Big Foot was in tears. He was like a boy, and the more he cried, the louder he cried, and the more painful it sounded.

The secret I had held for Big Foot was now shown to everybody.

Hat said, 'What, he crying?' And Hat laughed.

He seemed to forget all about the cow. He said, 'Well, well, look at man, eh!'

And all of us from Miguel Street laughed at Big Foot.

All except me. For I knew how he felt although he was a big man and I was a boy. I wished I had never betted that six cents with Boyee.

The papers next morning said, 'PUGILIST SOBS IN RING.'

Trinidad thought it was Big Foot, the comedian, doing something funny again.

But we knew otherwise.

Big Foot left Miguel Street, and the last I heard of him was that he was a labourer in a quarry in Laventille.

*

About six months later a little scandal was rippling through Trinidad, making everybody feel silly.

The R.A.F. champion, it turned out, had never been in the R.A.F., and as a boxer he was completely unknown.

Hat said, 'Well, what you expect in a place like this?'

8. The Pyrotechnicist

A STRANGER could drive through Miguel Street and just say 'Slum!' because he could see no more. But we, who lived there, saw our street as a world, where everybody was quite different from everybody else. Man-man was mad; George was stupid; Big Foot was a bully; Hat was an adventurer; Popo was a philosopher; and Morgan was our comedian.

Or that was how we looked upon him. But looking back now after so many years, I think he deserved a lot more respect than we gave him. It was his own fault, of course. He was one of those men who deliberately set out to clown and wasn't happy unless people were laughing at him, and he was always thinking of new crazinesses which he hoped would amuse us. He was the sort of man who, having once created a laugh by sticking the match in his mouth and trying to light it with his cigarette, having once done that, does it over and over again.

Hat used to say, 'Is a damn nuisance, having that man trying to be funny all the time, when all of us well know that he not so happy at all.'

I felt that sometimes Morgan knew his jokes were not coming off, and that made him so miserable that we all felt unkind and nasty.

Morgan was the first artist I ever met in my life. He spent nearly all his time, even when he was playing the fool, thinking about beauty. Morgan made fireworks. He loved fireworks, and he was full of theories about fireworks. Something about the Cosmic Dance or the Dance of Life. But this was the sort of talk that went clean over our heads in Miguel Street. And when Morgan saw this, he would begin using even bigger words. Just for the joke. One of the big words I learnt from Morgan is the title of this sketch.

But very few people in Trinidad used Morgan's fireworks. All the big fêtes in the island passed – Races, Carnival, Discovery Day, the Indian Centenary – and while the rest of the island was going crazy with rum and music and pretty women by the sea, Morgan was just going crazy with rage.

Morgan used to go to the Savannah and watch the fireworks of his rivals, and hear the cheers of the crowd as the fireworks spattered and spangled the sky. He would come in a great temper and beat all his children. He had ten of them. His wife was too big for him to beat.

Hat would say, 'We better send for the fire-brigade.'

And for the next two or three hours Morgan would prowl in a stupid sort of way around his back-yard, letting off fireworks so crazily that we used to hear his wife shouting, 'Morgan, stop playing the ass. You make ten children and you have a wife, and you can't afford to go and dead now.'

Morgan would roar like a bull and beat on the galvanized-iron fence.

He would shout, 'Everybody want to beat me. Everybody.'

Hat said, 'You know we hearing the real Morgan now.'

These fits of craziness made Morgan a real terror. When the fits were on him, he had the idea that Bhakcu, the mechanical genius who was my uncle, was always ready to beat him, and at about eleven o'clock in the evenings, the idea just seemed to explode in his head.

He would beat on the fence and shout, 'Bhakcu, you fat-belly good-for-nothing son-of-a-bitch, come out and fight like a man.'

Bhakcu would keep on reading the *Ramayana*, in his doleful singing voice; lying flat on his belly on his bed.

Bhakcu was a big man, and Morgan was a very small man, with the smallest hands and the thinnest wrists in Miguel Street.

Mrs Bhakcu would say, 'Morgan, why you don't shut up and go to sleep?'

Mrs Morgan would reply, 'Hey, you thin-foot woman! You better leave my husband alone, you hear. Why you don't look after your own?'

Mrs Bhakcu would say, 'You better mind your mouth. Otherwise I come up and turn your face with one slap, you hear.'

Mrs Bhakcu was four feet high, three feet wide, and three feet deep. Mrs Morgan was a little over six feet tall and built like a weight-lifter.

Mrs Morgan said, 'Why you don't get your big-belly husband to go and fix some more motor-car, and stop reading that damn stupid sing-song he always sing-songing?'

By this time Morgan would be on the pavement with us, laughing in a funny sort of way, saying, 'Hear them women and them!' He would drink some rum from a hip-flask and say, 'Just watch and see. You know the calypso?

> The more they try to do me bad
> Is the better I live in Trinidad.

Is the same thing with me, you know. This time so next year, I go have the King of England and the King of America paying me millions to make fireworks for them. The most beautiful fireworks anybody ever see.'

And Hat or somebody else would ask, 'You go make the fireworks for them?'

Morgan would say, 'Make *what*? Make nothing. By this time so next year, I go have the King of England and the King of America paying me millions to make fireworks for them. The most beautiful fireworks anybody ever see.'

And, in the meantime, in the back of the yard, Mrs Bhakcu was saying, '*He* have big belly. But what yours have? I don't know what yours going to sit on next year this time, you hear.'

And next morning Morgan was as straight and sober as ever, talking about his experiments.

This Morgan was more like a bird than a man. It was not only that he was as thin as a match-stick. He had a long neck that could swivel like a bird's. His eyes were bright and restless. And when he spoke it was in a pecking sort of way, as though he was not throwing out words, but picking up corn. He walked with a quick, tripping step, looking back over his shoulder at somebody following who wasn't there.

Hat said, 'You know how he get so? Is his wife, you know. He fraid she too bad. Spanish woman, you know. Full of blood and fire.'

Boyee said, 'You suppose that is why he want to make fireworks so?'

Hat said, 'People funny like hell. You never know with them.'

But Morgan used to make a joke of even his appearance, flinging out his arms and feet when he knew people were looking at him.

Morgan also made fun of his wife and his ten children. 'Is a miracle to me,' he said, 'that a man like me have ten children. I don't know how I manage it.'

Edward said, 'How you sure is your children?'

Morgan laughed, and said, 'I have my doubts.'

*

Hat didn't like Morgan. He said, 'Is hard to say. But it have something about him I can't really take. I always feel he overdoing everything. I always feel the man lying about everything. I feel that he even lying to hisself.'

The Pyrotechnicist

I don't think any of us understood what Hat meant. Morgan was becoming a little too troublesome, and it was hard for all of us to begin smiling as soon as we saw him, which was what he wanted.

Still his firework experiments continued and every now and then we heard an explosion from Morgan's house, and we saw the puffs of coloured smoke. This was one of the standing amusements of the street.

But as time went by and Morgan found that no one was willing to buy his fireworks, he began to make fun even of his fireworks. He was not content with the laughter of the street when there was an explosion in his house.

Hat said, 'When a man start laughing at something he fight for all the time, you don't know whether to laugh or cry.' And Hat decided that Morgan was just a fool.

I suppose it was because of Hat that we decided not to laugh at Morgan any more.

Hat said, 'It go make him stop playing the fool.'

But it didn't.

Morgan grew wilder than ever, and began challenging Bhakcu to fight about two or three times a week. He began beating his children more than ever.

And he made one last attempt to make us laugh.

I heard about it from Chris, Morgan's fourth son. We were in the café at the corner of Miguel Street.

Chris said, 'Is a crime to talk to you now, you know.'

I said, 'Don't tell me. Is the old man again?'

Chris nodded and he showed me a sheet of paper, headed CRIME AND PUNISHMENT.

Chris said with pride, 'Look at it.'

It was a long list, with entries like this:

For fighting	i) at home	Five strokes
	ii) in the street	Seven strokes
	iii) at school	Eight strokes

Chris looked at me and said in a very worried way, 'It funny like hell, eh? This sort of thing make blows a joke.'

I said yes, and asked, 'But you say is a crime to talk to me. Where it is?'

Chris showed me:

For talking to street rabs	Four strokes
For playing with street rabs	Eight strokes

I said, 'But your father don't mind talking to us. What wrong if you talk to us?'

Chris said, 'But this ain't nothing at all. You must come on Sunday and see what happen.'

I could see that Chris was pleased as anything.

About six of us went that Sunday. Morgan was there to meet us and he took us into his drawing-room. Then he disappeared. There were many chairs and benches as though there was going to be a concert. Morgan's eldest son was standing at a little table in the corner.

Suddenly this boy said, 'Stand!'

We all stood up, and Morgan appeared, smiling all round.

I asked Hat, 'Why he smiling so?'

Hat said, 'That is how the magistrates and them does smile when they come in court.'

Morgan's eldest son shouted, 'Andrew Morgan!'

Andrew Morgan came and stood before his father.

The eldest boy read very loudly, 'Andrew Morgan, you are charged with stoning the tamarind tree in Miss Dorothy's yard; you are charged with ripping off three buttons for the purpose of purchasing some marbles; you are charged with fighting Dorothy Morgan; you are charged with stealing two *tolums* and three sugar-cakes. Do you plead guilty or not guilty?'

Andrew said, 'Guilty.'

Morgan, scribbling on a sheet of paper, looked up.

'Have you anything to say?'

Andrew said, 'I sorry, sir.'

Morgan said, 'We will let the sentences run concurrently. Twelve strokes.'

One by one, the Morgan children were judged and sentenced. Even the eldest boy had to receive some punishment.

Morgan then rose and said, 'These sentences will be carried out this afternoon.'

He smiled all round, and left the room.

*

The joke misfired completely.

Hat said, 'Nah, nah, man, you can't make fun of your own self and your own children that way, and invite all the street to see. Nah, it ain't right.'

I felt the joke was somehow terrible and frightening.

And when Morgan came out on the pavement that evening, his face fixed in a smile, he got none of the laughter he had expected. Nobody ran up to him and clapped him on the back, saying, 'But this man Morgan really mad, you hear. You hear how he beating his children these days . . .?' No one said anything like that. No one said anything to him.

It was easy to see he was shattered.

Morgan got really drunk that night and challenged everybody to fight. He even challenged me.

Mrs Morgan had padlocked the front gate, so Morgan could only run about in his yard. He was as mad as a mad bull, bellowing and butting at the fence. He kept saying over and over again, 'You people think I not a man, eh? My father had eight children. I is his son. I have ten. I better than all of you put together.'

Hat said, 'He soon go start crying and then he go sleep.'

But I spent a lot of time that night before going to sleep thinking about Morgan, feeling sorry for him because of that little devil he had inside him. For that was what I thought was wrong with him. I fancied that inside him was a red, grinning devil pricking Morgan with his fork.

*

Mrs Morgan and the children went to the country.

Morgan no longer came out to the pavement, seeking our company. He was busy with his experiments. There were a series of minor explosions and lots of smoke.

Apart from that, peace reigned in our end of Miguel Street.

I wondered what Morgan was doing and thinking in all that solitude.

The following Sunday it rained heavily, and everyone was forced to go to bed early. The street was wet and glistening, and by eleven there was no noise save for the patter of the rain on the corrugated-iron roofs.

A short, sharp shout cracked through the street, and got us up.

I could hear windows being flung open, and I heard people saying, 'What happen? What happen?'

'Is Morgan. Is Morgan. Something happening by Morgan.'

I was already out in the street and in front of Morgan's house. I never slept in pyjamas. I wasn't in that class.

The first thing I saw in the darkness of Morgan's yard was the figure of a woman hurrying away from the house to the back gate that opened on to the sewage trace between Miguel Street and Alfonso Street.

It was drizzling now, not very hard, and in no time at all quite a crowd had joined me.

It was all a bit mysterious — the shout, the woman disappearing, the dark house.

Then we heard Mrs Morgan shouting, 'Teresa Blake, Teresa Blake, what you doing with my man?' It was a cry of great pain.

Mrs Bhakcu was at my side. 'I always know about this Teresa, but I keep my mouth shut.'

Bhakcu said, 'Yes, you know everything, like your mother.'

A light came on in the house.

Then it went off again.

We heard Mrs Morgan saying, 'Why you fraid the light so for? Ain't you is man? Put the light on, let we see the great big man you is.'

The light went on; then off again.

We heard Morgan's voice, but it was so low we couldn't make out what he was saying.

Mrs Morgan said, 'Yes, hero.' And the light came on again.

We heard Morgan mumbling again.

Mrs Morgan said, 'No, hero.'

The light went off; then it went on.

Mrs Morgan was saying, 'Leave the light on. Come, let we show the big big hero to the people in the street. Come, let we show them what man really make like. You is not a antiman, you is real man. You ain't only make ten children with me, you going to make more with somebody else.'

We heard Morgan's voice, a fluting unhappy thing.

Mrs Morgan said, 'But what you fraid now for? Ain't you is the funny man? The clown? Come, let them see see the clown and the big man you is. Let them see what man really make like.'

Morgan was wailing by this time, and trying to talk.

Mrs Morgan was saying, 'If you try to put that light off, I break up your little thin tail like a match-stick here, you hear.'

Then the front door was flung open, and we saw.

Mrs Morgan was holding up Morgan by his waist. He was

practically naked, and he looked so thin, he was like a boy with an old man's face. He wasn't looking at us, but at Mrs Morgan's face, and he was squirming in her grasp, trying to get away. But Mrs Morgan was a strong woman.

Mrs Morgan was looking not at us, but at the man in her arm.

She was saying, 'But this is the big man I have, eh? So this is the man I married and slaving all my life for?' And then she began laughing, in a croaking, nasty way.

She looked at us for a moment, and said, 'Well, laugh now. He don't mind. He always want people to laugh at him.'

And the sight was so comic, the thin man held up so easily by the fat woman, that we did laugh. It was the sort of laugh that begins gently and then builds up into a bellowing belly laugh.

For the first time since he came to Miguel Street, Morgan was really being laughed at by the people.

*

And it broke him completely.

All the next day we waited for him to come out to the pavement, to congratulate him with our laughter. But we didn't see him.

Hat said, 'When I was little, my mother used to tell me, "Boy, you laughing all day. I bet you, you go cry tonight."'

*

That night my sleep was again disturbed. By shouts and sirens.

I looked through the window and saw a red sky and red smoke. Morgan's house was on fire.

And what a fire! Photographers from the papers were climbing up into other people's houses to get their pictures, and people were looking at them and not at the fire. Next morning there was a first-class picture with me part of the crowd in the top right-hand corner.

But what a fire it was! It was the most beautiful fire in Port of

Spain since 1933 when the Treasury (of all places) burnt down, and the calypsonian sang:

> It was a glorious and a beautiful scenery
> Was the burning of the Treasury.

What really made the fire beautiful was Morgan's fireworks going off. Then for the first time everybody saw the astonishing splendour of Morgan's fireworks. People who used to scoff at Morgan felt a little silly. I have travelled in many countries since, but I have seen nothing to beat the fireworks show in Morgan's house that night.

But Morgan made no more fireworks.

Hat said, 'When I was a little boy, my mother used to say, "If a man want something, and he want it really bad, he does get it, but when he get it he don't like it."'

Both of Morgan's ambitions were fulfilled. People laughed at him, and they still do. And he made the most beautiful fireworks in the world. But as Hat said, when a man gets something he wants badly, he doesn't like it.

*

As we expected, the thing came out in court. Morgan was charged with arson. The newspaper people had a lot of fun with Morgan, within the libel laws. One headline I remember: *Pyrotechnist Alleged Pyromaniac.*

But I was glad, though, that Morgan got off.

They said Morgan went to Venezuela. They said he went mad. They said he became a jockey in Colombia. They said all sorts of things, but the people of Miguel Street were always romancers.

9. Titus Hoyt, I.A.

THIS MAN WAS born to be an active and important member of a local road board in the country. An unkind fate had placed him in the city. He was a natural guide, philosopher and friend to anyone who stopped to listen.

Titus Hoyt was the first man I met when I came to Port of Spain, a year or two before the war.

My mother had fetched me from Chaguanas after my father died. We travelled up by train and took a bus to Miguel Street. It was the first time I had travelled in a city bus.

I said to my mother, 'Ma, look, they forget to ring the bell here.'

My mother said, 'If you ring the bell you damn well going to get off and walk home by yourself, you hear.'

And then a little later I said, 'Ma, look, the sea.'

People in the bus began to laugh.

My mother was really furious.

Early next morning my mother said, 'Look now, I giving you four cents. Go to the shop on the corner of this road, Miguel Street, and buy two hops bread for a cent apiece, and buy a penny butter. And come back quick.'

I found the shop and I bought the bread and butter – the red, salty type of butter.

Then I couldn't find my way back.

I found about six Miguel Streets, but none seemed to have my house. After a long time walking up and down I began to cry. I sat down on the pavement, and got my shoes wet in the gutter.

Some little white girls were playing in a yard behind me. I looked at them, still crying. A girl wearing a pink frock came out and said, 'Why you crying?'

I said, 'I lost.'

She put her hands on my shoulder and said, 'Don't cry. You know where you live?'

I pulled out a piece of paper from my shirt pocket and showed her. Then a man came up. He was wearing white shorts and a white shirt, and he looked funny.

The man said, 'Why he crying?' In a gruff, but interested way.

The girl told him.

The man said, 'I will take him home.'

I asked the girl to come too.

The man said, 'Yes, you better come to explain to his mother.'

The girl said, 'All right, Mr Titus Hoyt.'

That was one of the first things about Titus Hoyt that I found interesting. The girl calling him 'Mr Titus Hoyt'. Not Titus, or Mr Hoyt, but Mr Titus Hoyt. I later realized that everyone who knew him called him that.

When we got home the girl explained to my mother what had happened, and my mother was ashamed of me.

Then the girl left.

Mr Titus Hoyt looked at me and said, 'He look like a intelligent little boy.'

My mother said in a sarcastic way, 'Like his father.'

Titus Hoyt said, 'Now, young man, if a herring and a half cost a penny and a half, what's the cost of three herrings?'

Even in the country, in Chaguanas, we had heard about that.

Without waiting, I said, 'Three pennies.'

Titus Hoyt regarded me with wonder.

He told my mother, 'This boy bright like anything, ma'am.

You must take care of him and send him to a good school and feed him good food so he could study well.'

My mother didn't say anything.

When Titus Hoyt left, he said, 'Cheerio!'

That was the second interesting thing about him.

My mother beat me for getting my shoes wet in the gutter but she said she wouldn't beat me for getting lost.

For the rest of that day I ran about the yard saying, 'Cheerio! Cheerio!' to a tune of my own.

That evening Titus Hoyt came again.

My mother didn't seem to mind.

To me Titus Hoyt said, 'You can read?'

I said yes.

'And write?'

I said yes.

'Well, look,' he said, 'get some paper and a pencil and write what I tell you.'

I said, 'Paper and pencil?'

He nodded.

I ran to the kitchen and said, 'Ma, you got any paper and pencil?'

My mother said, 'What you think I is? A shopkeeper?'

Titus Hoyt shouted, 'Is for me, ma'am.'

My mother said, 'Oh.' In a disappointed way.

She said, 'In the bottom drawer of the bureau you go find my purse. It have a pencil in it.'

And she gave me a copy-book from the kitchen shelf.

Mr Titus Hoyt said, 'Now, young man, write. Write the address of this house in the top right-hand corner, and below that, the date.' Then he asked, 'You know who we writing this letter to, boy?'

I shook my head.

He said, 'Ha, boy! Ha! We writing to the *Guardian*, boy.'

I said, 'The *Trinidad Guardian*? The paper? What, *me* writing to the *Guardian*! But only big big man does write to the *Guardian*.'

Titus Hoyt smiled. 'That's *why* you writing. It go surprise them.'

I said, 'What I go write to them about?'

He said, 'You go write it now. Write. To the Editor, *Trinidad Guardian*. Dear Sir, I am but a child of eight (How old you is? Well, it don't matter anyway) and yesterday my mother sent me to make a purchase in the city. This, dear Mr Editor, was my first peregrination p-e-r-e-g-r-i-n-a-t-i-o-n in this metropolis, and I had the misfortune to wander from the path my mother had indicated – '

I said, 'Oh God, Mr Titus Hoyt, where you learn all these big words and them? You sure you spelling them right?'

Titus Hoyt smiled. 'I spend all afternoon making up this letter,' he said.

I wrote: ' . . . and in this state of despair I was rescued by a Mr Titus Hoyt, of Miguel Street. This only goes to show, dear Mr Editor, that human kindness is a quality not yet extinct in this world.'

The *Guardian* never printed the letter.

When I next saw Titus Hoyt, he said, 'Well, never mind. One day, boy, one day, I go make them sit up and take notice of every word I say. Just wait and see.'

And before he left, he said, 'Drinking your milk?'

He had persuaded my mother to give me half a pint of milk every day. Milk was good for the brains.

It is one of the sadnesses of my life that I never fulfilled Titus Hoyt's hopes for my academic success.

I still remember with tenderness the interest he took in me. Sometimes his views clashed with my mother's. There was the business of the cobwebs, for instance.

Boyee, with whom I had become friendly very quickly, was

teaching me to ride. I had fallen and cut myself nastily on the shin.

My mother was attempting to cure this with sooty cobwebs soaked in rum.

Titus Hoyt was horrified. 'You ain't know what you doing,' he shouted.

My mother said, 'Mr Titus Hoyt, I will kindly ask you to mind your own business. The day you make a baby yourself I go listen to what you have to say.'

Titus Hoyt refused to be ridiculed. He said, 'Take the boy to the doctor, man.'

I was watching them argue, not caring greatly either way.

In the end I went to the doctor.

Titus Hoyt reappeared in a new role.

He told my mother, 'For the last two three months I been taking the first-aid course with the Red Cross. I go dress the boy foot for you.'

That really terrified me.

For about a month or so afterwards, people in Miguel Street could tell when it was nine o'clock in the morning. By my shrieks. Titus Hoyt loved his work.

All this gives some clue to the real nature of the man.

The next step followed naturally.

Titus Hoyt began to teach.

It began in a small way, after the fashion of all great enterprises.

He had decided to sit for the external arts degree of London University. He began to learn Latin, teaching himself, and as fast as he learned, he taught us.

He rounded up three or four of us and taught us in the verandah of his house. He kept chickens in his yard and the place stank.

That Latin stage didn't last very long. We got as far as the fourth declension, and then Boyee and Errol and myself began asking questions. They were not the sort of questions Titus Hoyt liked.

Boyee said, 'Mr Titus Hoyt, I think you making up all this, you know, making it up as you go on.'

Titus Hoyt said, 'But I telling you, I not making it up. Look, here it is in black and white.'

Errol said, 'I feel, Mr Titus Hoyt, that one man sit down one day and make all this up and have everybody else learning it.'

Titus Hoyt asked me, 'What is the accusative singular of *bellum*?'

Feeling wicked, because I was betraying him, I said to Titus Hoyt, 'Mr Titus Hoyt, when you was my age, how you woulda feel if somebody did ask you that question?'

And then Boyee asked, 'Mr Titus Hoyt, what is the meaning of the ablative case?'

So the Latin lessons ended.

*

But however much we laughed at him, we couldn't deny that Titus Hoyt was a deep man.

Hat used to say, 'He is a thinker, that man.'

Titus Hoyt thought about all sorts of things, and he thought dangerous things sometimes.

Hat said, 'I don't think Titus Hoyt like God, you know.'

Titus Hoyt would say, 'The thing that really matter is faith. Look, I believe that if I pull out this bicycle-lamp from my pocket here, and set it up somewhere, and really really believe in it and pray to it, what I pray for go come. That is what I believe.'

And so saying he would rise and leave, not forgetting to say, 'Cheerio!'

He had the habit of rushing up to us and saying, 'Silence, everybody. I just been thinking. Listen to what I just been thinking.'

One day he rushed up and said, 'I been thinking how this war could end. If Europe could just sink for five minutes all the Germans go drown – '

Eddoes said, 'But England go drown too.'

Titus Hoyt agreed and looked sad. 'I lose my head, man,' he said. 'I lose my head.'

And he wandered away, muttering to himself, and shaking his head.

One day he cycled right up to us when we were talking about the Barbados-Trinidad cricket match. Things were not going well for Trinidad and we were worried.

Titus Hoyt rushed up and said, 'Silence. I just been thinking. Look, boys, it ever strike you that the world not real at all? It ever strike you that we have the only mind in the world and you just thinking up everything else? Like me here, having the only mind in the world, and thinking up you people here, thinking up the war and all the houses and the ships and them in the harbour. That ever cross your mind?'

*

His interest in teaching didn't die.

We often saw him going about with big books. These books were about teaching.

Titus Hoyt used to say, 'Is a science, man. The trouble with Trinidad is that the teachers don't have this science of teaching.'

And, 'Is the biggest thing in the world, man. Having the minds of the young to train. Think of that. Think.'

It soon became clear that whatever we thought about it Titus Hoyt was bent on training our minds.

He formed the Miguel Street Literary and Social Youth Club, and had it affiliated to the Trinidad and Tobago Youth Association.

We used to meet in his house which was well supplied with things to eat and drink. The walls of his house were now hung with improving quotations, some typed, some cut out of magazines and pasted on bits of cardboard.

I also noticed a big thing called 'Time-table'.

From this I gathered that Titus Hoyt was to rise at five-thirty, read Something from Greek philosophers until six, spend fifteen minutes bathing and exercising, another five reading the morning paper, and ten on breakfast. It was a formidable thing altogether.

Titus Hoyt said, 'If I follow the time-table I will be a educated man in about three four years.'

The Miguel Street Club didn't last very long.

It was Titus Hoyt's fault.

No man in his proper senses would have made Boyee secretary. Most of Boyee's minutes consisted of the names of people present.

And then we all had to write and read something.

The Miguel Street Literary and Social Club became nothing more than a gathering of film critics.

Titus Hoyt said, 'No, man. We just can't have all you boys talking about pictures all the time. I will have to get some propaganda for you boys.'

Boyee said, 'Mr Titus Hoyt, what we want with propaganda? Is a German thing.'

Titus Hoyt smiled. 'That is not the proper meaning of the word, boy. I am using the word in it proper meaning. Is education, boy, that makes me know things like that.'

Boyee was sent as our delegate to the Youth Association annual conference.

When he came back Boyee said, 'Is a helluva thing at that youth conference. Is only a pack of old, old people it have there.'

The attraction of the Coca-Cola and the cakes and the ice-cream began to fade. Some of us began staying away from meetings.

Titus Hoyt made one last effort to keep the club together.

One day he said, 'Next Sunday the club will go on a visit to Fort George.'

There were cries of disapproval.

Titus Hoyt said, 'You see, you people don't care about your country. How many of you know about Fort George? Not one of you here know about the place. But is history, man, your history, and you must learn about things like that. You must remember that the boys and girls of today are the men and women of tomorrow. The old Romans had a saying, you know. *Mens sana in corpore sano.* I think we will make the walk to Fort George.'

Still no one wanted to go.

Titus Hoyt said, 'At the top of Fort George it have a stream, and it cool cool and the water crystal clear. You could bathe there when we get to the top.'

We couldn't resist that.

The next Sunday a whole group of us took the trolley-bus to Mucurapo.

When the conductor came round to collect the fares, Titus Hoyt said, 'Come back a little later.' And he paid the conductor only when we got off the bus. The fare for everybody came up to about two shillings. But Titus Hoyt gave the conductor a shilling, saying, 'We don't want any ticket, man!' The conductor and Titus Hoyt laughed.

It was a long walk up the hill, red and dusty, and hot.

Titus Hoyt told us, 'This fort was built at a time when the French and them was planning to invade Trinidad.'

We gasped.

We had never realized that anyone considered us so important.

Titus Hoyt said, 'That was in 1803, when we was fighting Napoleon.'

We saw a few old rusty guns at the side of the path and heaps of rusty cannon-balls.

I asked, 'The French invade Trinidad, Mr Titus Hoyt?'

Titus Hoyt shook his head in a disappointed way. 'No, they didn't attack. But we was ready, man. Ready for them.'

Boyee said, 'You sure it have this stream up there you tell us about, Mr Titus Hoyt?'

Titus Hoyt said, 'What you think I is? A liar?'

Boyee said, 'I ain't saying nothing.'

We walked and sweated. Boyee took off his shoes.

Errol said, 'If it ain't have that stream up there, somebody going to catch hell.'

We got to the top, had a quick look at the graveyard where there were a few tombstones of British soldiers dead long ago; and we looked through the telescope at the city of Port of Spain large and sprawling beneath us. We could see the people walking in the streets as large as life.

Then we went looking for the stream.

We couldn't find it.

Titus Hoyt said, 'It must be here somewhere. When I was a boy I use to bathe in it.'

Boyee said, 'And what happen now? It dry up?'

Titus Hoyt said, 'It look so.'

Boyee got really mad, and you couldn't blame him. It was hard work coming up that hill, and we were all hot and thirsty.

He insulted Titus Hoyt in a very crude way.

Titus Hoyt said, 'Remember, Boyee, you are the secretary of the Miguel Street Literary and Social Club. Remember that you have just attended a meeting of the Youth Association as our delegate. Remember these things.'

Boyee said, 'Go to hell, Hoyt.'

We were aghast.

So the Literary Club broke up.

*

It wasn't long after that Titus Hoyt got his Inter Arts degree and set up a school of his own. He had a big sign placed in his garden:

TITUS HOYT, I.A. (London, External)
Passes in the Cambridge
School Certificate Guaranteed

One year the *Guardian* had a brilliant idea. They started the Needy Cases Fund to help needy cases at Christmas. It was popular and after a few years was called The Neediest Cases Fund. At the beginning of November the *Guardian* announced the target for the fund and it was a daily excitement until Christmas Eve to see how the fund rose. It was always front page news and everybody who gave got his name in the papers.

In the middle of December one year, when the excitement was high, Miguel Street was in the news.

Hat showed us the paper and we read:

FOLLOW THE EXAMPLE OF THIS TINYMITE!

The smallest and most touching response to our appeal to bring Yuletide cheer to the unfortunate has come in a letter from Mr Titus Hoyt, I.A., a headmaster of Miguel Street, Port of Spain. The letter was sent to Mr Hoyt by one of his pupils who wishes to remain anonymous. We have Mr Hoyt's permission to print the letter in full.

'Dear Mr Hoyt, I am only eight and, as you doubtless know, I am a member of the GUARDIAN Tinymites League. I read Aunt Juanita every Sunday. You, dear Mr Hoyt, have always extolled the virtue of charity and you have spoken repeatedly of the fine work the GUARDIAN Neediest Cases Fund is doing to bring Yuletide cheer to the unfortunate. I have decided to yield to your earnest entreaty. I have very little money to offer – a mere six cents, in fact, but take it, Mr Hoyt, and send it to the GUARDIAN Neediest Cases Fund. May it bring Yuletide cheer to some poor unfortunate! I know it is not much. But, like the widow, I give my mite. I remain, dear Mr Hoyt, One of Your Pupils.'

And there was a large photograph of Titus Hoyt, smiling and pop-eyed in the flash of the camera.

10. The Maternal Instinct

I suppose Laura holds a world record.

Laura had eight children.

There is nothing surprising in that.

These eight children had seven fathers.

Beat that!

It was Laura who gave me my first lesson in biology. She lived just next door to us, and I found myself observing her closely.

I would notice her belly rising for months.

Then I would miss her for a short time.

And the next time I saw her she would be quite flat.

And the leavening process would begin again in a few months.

To me this was one of the wonders of the world in which I lived, and I always observed Laura. She herself was quite gay about what was happening to her. She used to point to it, and say, 'This thing happening again, but you get use to it after the first three four times. Is a damn nuisance, though.'

She used to blame God, and speak about the wickedness of men.

For her first six children she tried six different men.

Hat used to say, 'Some people hard to please.'

But I don't want to give you the impression that Laura spent all her time having babies and decrying men, and generally feeling sorry for herself. If Bogart was the most bored person in the street,

Laura was the most vivacious. She was always gay, and she liked me.

She would give me plums and mangoes when she had them; and whenever she made sugar-cakes she would give me some.

Even my mother, who had a great dislike of laughter, especially in me, even my mother used to laugh at Laura.

She often said to me, 'I don't know why Laura muching you up so for. Like she ain't have enough children to mind.'

I think my mother was right. I don't think a woman like Laura could have ever had too many children. She loved all her children, though you wouldn't have believed it from the language she used when she spoke to them. Some of Laura's shouts and curses were the richest things I have ever heard, and I shall never forget them.

Hat said once, 'Man, she like Shakespeare when it come to using words.'

Laura used to shout, 'Alwyn, you broad-mouth brute, come here.'

And, 'Gavin, if you don't come here this minute, I make you fart fire, you hear.'

And, 'Lorna, you black bow-leg bitch, why you can't look what you doing?'

*

Now, to compare Laura, the mother of eight, with Mary the Chinese, also mother of eight, doesn't seem fair. Because Mary took really good care of her children and never spoke harshly to them. But Mary, mark you, had a husband who owned a shop, and Mary could afford to be polite and nice to her children, after stuffing them full of chop-suey and chow-min, and chow-fan, and things with names like that. But who could Laura look to for money to keep her children?

The men who cycled slowly past Laura's house in the evening, whistling for Laura, were not going to give any of their money to Laura's children. They just wanted Laura.

I asked my mother, 'How Laura does live?'

My mother slapped me, saying, 'You know, you too fast for a little boy.'

I suspected the worst.

But I wouldn't have liked that to be true.

So I asked Hat. Hat said, 'She have a lot of friends who does sell in the market. They does give she things free, and sometimes one or two or three of she husbands does give she something too, but that not much.'

The oddest part of the whole business was Laura herself. Laura was no beauty. As Boyee said one day, 'She have a face like the top of a motor-car battery.' And she was a little more than plump.

I am talking now of the time when she had had only six children.

*

One day Hat said, 'Laura have a new man.'

Everybody laughed, 'Stale news. If Laura have she way, she go try every man once.'

But Hat said, 'No, is serious. He come to live with she for good now. I see him this morning when I was taking out the cows.'

We watched and waited for this man.

We later learned that he was watching and waiting for us.

In no time at all this man, Nathaniel, had become one of the gang in Miguel Street. But it was clear that he was not really one of us. He came from the east end of Port of Spain, which we considered dirtier; and his language was really coarse.

He made out that he was a kind of terror in the east end around Piccadilly Street. He told many stories about gang-fights, and he let it be known that he had disfigured two or three people.

Hat said, 'I think he lying like hell, you know.'

I distrusted him myself. He was a small man, and I always felt that small men were more likely to be wicked and violent.

But what really sickened us was his attitude to women. We were none of us chivalrous, but Nathaniel had a contempt for women which we wouldn't like. He would make rude remarks when women passed.

Nathaniel would say, 'Women just like cows. Cow and they is the same thing.'

And when Miss Ricaud, the welfare woman, passed, Nathaniel would say, 'Look at that big cow.'

Which wasn't in good taste, for we all thought that Miss Ricaud was too fat to be laughed at, and ought instead to be pitied.

Nathaniel, in the early stages, tried to make us believe that he knew how to keep Laura in her place. He hinted that he used to beat her. He used to say, 'Woman and them like a good dose of blows, you know. You know the calypso:

> Every now and then just knock them down.
> Every now and then just throw them down.
> Black up their eye and bruise up their knee
> And then they love you eternally.

Is gospel truth about woman.'

Hat said, 'Woman is a funny thing, for truth, though. I don't know what a woman like Laura see in Nathaniel.'

Eddoes said, 'I know a helluva lot about woman. I think Nathaniel lying like hell. I think when he with Laura he got his tail between his legs all the time.'

We used to hear fights and hear the children screaming all over the place, and when we saw Nathaniel, he would just say, 'Just been beating some sense into that woman.'

Hat said, 'Is a funny thing. Laura don't look any sadder.'

Nathaniel said, 'Is only blows she really want to keep she happy.'

Nathaniel was lying of course. It wasn't he who was giving the blows, it was Laura. That came out the day when Nathaniel tried to wear a hat to cover up a beaten eye.

Eddoes said, 'It look like they make up that calypso about men, not women.'

Nathaniel tried to get at Eddoes, who was small and thin. But Hat said, 'Go try that on Laura. I know Laura. Laura just trying not to beat you up too bad just to keep you with she, but the day she start getting tired of you, you better run, boy.'

We prayed for something to happen to make Nathaniel leave Miguel Street.

Hat said, 'We ain't have to wait long. Laura making baby eight months now. Another month, and Nathaniel gone.'

Eddoes said, 'That would be a real record. Seven children with seven different man.'

The baby came.

It was on a Saturday. Just the evening before I had seen Laura standing in her yard leaning on the fence.

The baby came at eight o'clock in the morning. And, like a miracle, just two hours later, Laura was calling across to my mother.

I hid and looked.

Laura was leaning on her window-sill. She was eating a mango, and the yellow juice was smeared all over her face.

She was saying to my mother, 'The baby come this morning.'

And my mother only said, 'Boy or girl?'

Laura said, 'What sort of luck you think I have? It looks like I really blight. Is another girl. I just thought I would let you know, that's all. Well, I got to go now. I have to do some sewing.'

And that very evening it looked as though what Hat said was going to come true. For that evening Laura came out to the pavement and shouted to Nathaniel, 'Hey, Nathaniel, come here.'

Hat said, 'But what the hell is this? Ain't is this morning she make baby?'

Nathaniel tried to show off to us. He said to Laura, 'I busy. I ain't coming.'

Laura advanced, and I could see fight in her manner. She said, 'You ain't coming? Ain't coming? But what is this I hearing?'

Nathaniel was worried. He tried to talk to us, but he wasn't talking in a sensible way.

Laura said, 'You think you is a man. But don't try playing man with me, you hear. Yes, Nathaniel, is you I talking to, you with your bottom like two stale bread in you pants.'

This was one of Laura's best, and we all began laughing. When she saw us laughing, Laura burst out too.

Hat said, 'This woman is a real case.'

*

But even after the birth of his baby Nathaniel didn't leave Miguel Street. We were a little worried.

Hat said, 'If she don't look out she go have another baby with the same man, you know.'

It wasn't Laura's fault that Nathaniel didn't go. She knocked him about a lot, and did so quite openly now. Sometimes she locked him out, and then we would hear Nathaniel crying and coaxing from the pavement, 'Laura, darling, Laura, *doux-doux*, just let me come in tonight. Laura, *doux-doux*, let me come in.'

He had dropped all pretence now of keeping Laura in her place. He no longer sought our company, and we were glad of that.

Hat used to say, 'I don't know why he don't go back to the Dry River where he come from. They ain't have any culture there, and he would be happier.'

I couldn't understand why he stayed.

Hat said, 'It have some man like that. They like woman to kick them around.'

And Laura was getting angrier with Nathaniel.

One day we heard her tell him, 'You think because you give me one baby, you own me. That baby only come by accident, you hear.'

She threatened to get the police.

Nathaniel said, 'But who go mind your children?'

Laura said, 'That is my worry. I don't want you here. You is only another mouth to feed. And if you don't leave me right right now I go go and call Sergeant Charles for you.'

It was this threat of the police that made Nathaniel leave.

He was in tears.

But Laura was swelling out again.

Hat said, 'Oh, God! Two babies by the same man!'

*

One of the miracles of life in Miguel Street was that no one starved. If you sit down at a table with pencil and paper and try to work it out, you will find it impossible. But I lived in Miguel Street, and can assure you that no one starved. Perhaps they did go hungry, but you never heard about it.

Laura's children grew.

The eldest daughter, Lorna, began working as a servant in a house in St Clair and took typing lessons from a man in Sackville Street.

Laura used to say, 'It have nothing like education in the world. I don't want my children to grow like me.'

In time, Laura delivered her eighth baby, as effortlessly as usual.

That baby was her last.

It wasn't that she was tired or that she had lost her love of the human race or lost her passion for adding to it. As a matter of fact, Laura never seemed to grow any older or less cheerful. I always felt that, given the opportunity, she could just go on and on having babies.

*

The eldest daughter, Lorna, came home from her typing lessons late one night and said, 'Ma, I going to make a baby.'

I heard the shriek that Laura gave.

And for the first time I heard Laura crying. It wasn't ordinary crying. She seemed to be crying all the cry she had saved up since she was born; all the cry she had tried to cover up with her laughter. I have heard people cry at funerals, but there is a lot of showing-off in their crying. Laura's crying that night was the most terrible thing I had heard. It made me feel that the world was a stupid, sad place, and I almost began crying with Laura.

All the street heard Laura crying.

Next day Boyee said, 'I don't see why she so mad about that. She does do the same.'

Hat got so annoyed that he took off his leather belt and beat Boyee.

I didn't know who I felt sorrier for – Laura or her daughter.

I felt that Laura was ashamed now to show herself in the street. When I did see her I found it hard to believe that she was the same woman who used to laugh with me and give me sugar-cakes.

She was an old woman now.

She no longer shouted at her children, no longer beat them. I don't know whether she was taking especial care of them or whether she had lost interest in them.

But we never heard Laura say a word of reproach to Lorna.

That was terrible.

Lorna brought her baby home. There were no jokes about it in the street.

Laura's house was a dead, silent house.

Hat said, 'Life is helluva thing. You can see trouble coming and you can't do a damn thing to prevent it coming. You just got to sit and watch and wait.'

*

According to the papers, it was just another week-end tragedy, one of many.

Lorna was drowned at Carenage.

Hat said, 'Is what they always do, swim out and out until they tired and can't swim no more.'

And when the police came to tell Laura about it, she had said very little.

Laura said, 'It good. It good. It better that way.'

11. The Blue Cart

THERE WERE MANY reasons why I wanted to be like Eddoes when I grew up.

He was one of the aristocrats of the street. He drove a scavenging-cart and so worked only in the mornings.

Then, as everybody said, Eddoes was a real 'saga-boy'. This didn't mean that he wrote epic poetry. It meant that he was a 'sweet-man', a man of leisure, well-dressed, and keen on women.

Hat used to say, 'For a man who does drive a scavenging-cart, this Eddoes too clean, you hear.'

Eddoes was crazy about cleanliness.

He used to brush his teeth for hours.

In fact, if you were telling a stranger about Eddoes you would say, 'You know – the little fellow with a tooth-brush always in his mouth.'

This was one thing in Eddoes I really admired. Once I stuck a tooth-brush in my mouth and walked about our yard in the middle of the day.

My mother said, 'You playing man? But why you don't wait until your pee make froth?'

That made me miserable for days.

But it didn't prevent me taking the tooth-brush to school and wearing it there. It caused quite a stir. But I quickly realized that only a man like Eddoes could have worn a tooth-brush and carried it off.

Eddoes was always well-dressed. His khaki trousers were always creased and his shoes always shone. He wore his shirts with three buttons undone so you could see his hairy chest. His shirt cuffs were turned up just above the wrist and you could see his gold wrist-watch.

Even when Eddoes wore a coat you saw the watch. From the way he wore the coat you thought that Eddoes hadn't realized that the end of the coat-sleeve had been caught in the watch-strap.

It was only when I grew up I realized how small and how thin Eddoes really was.

I asked Hat, 'You think is true all this talk Eddoes giving us about how woman running after him?'

Hat said, 'Well, boy, woman these days funny like hell. They go run after a dwarf if he got money.'

I said, 'I don't believe you.'

I was very young at the time.

But I always thought, 'If it have one man in this world woman bound to like, that man is Eddoes.'

He sat on his blue cart with so much grace. And how smart that tooth-brush was in his mouth!

But you couldn't talk to him when he was on his cart. Then he was quite different from the Eddoes we knew on the ground, then he never laughed, but was always serious. And if we tried to ride on the back of his cart, as we used to on the back of the ice-cart, Eddoes would crack his whip at us in a nasty way, and shout, 'What sort of cart you think this is? Your father can't buy cart like this, you hear?'

Every year Eddoes won the City Council's award for the cleanest scavenging-cart.

And to hear Eddoes talk about his job was to make yourself feel sad and inferior.

He said he knew everybody important in Port of Spain, from the Governor down.

He would say, 'Collected two three tins of rubbish from the Director of Medical Services yesterday. I know him good, you know. Been collecting his rubbish for years, ever since he was a little doctor in Woodbrook, catching hell. So I see him yesterday and he say, "Eddoes (that is how he does always call me, you know) Eddoes," he say, "come and have a drink." Well, when I working I don't like drinking because it does keep you back. But he nearly drag me off the cart, man. In the end I had to drink with him. He tell me all his troubles.'

There were also stories of rich women waiting for him behind rubbish tins, women begging Eddoes to take away their rubbish.

But you should have seen Eddoes on those days when the scavengers struck. As I have told you already, these scavengers were proud people and stood for no nonsense from anybody.

They knew they had power. They could make Port of Spain stink in twenty-four hours if they struck.

On these important days Eddoes would walk slowly and thoughtfully up and down Miguel Street. He looked grim then, and fierce, and he wouldn't speak to a soul.

He wore a red scarf and a tooth-brush with a red handle on these days.

Sometimes we went to Woodford Square to the strike meeting, to gaze at these exciting people.

It amazed me to see Eddoes singing. The songs were violent, but Eddoes looked so sad.

Hat told me, 'It have detectives here, you know. They taking down every word Eddoes and them saying.'

It was easy to recognize the detectives. They were wearing a sort of plain clothes uniform – brown hats, white shirts, and brown trousers. They were writing in big note-books with red pencils.

And Eddoes didn't look scared!

We all knew that Eddoes wasn't a man to be played with.

*

You couldn't blame Eddoes then for being proud.

One day Eddoes brought home a pair of shoes and showed it to us in a quiet way, as though he wasn't really interested whether we looked at the shoes or not.

He said, brushing his teeth, and looking away from us, 'Got these shoes today from the *labasse*, the dump, you know. They was just lying there and I pick them up.'

We whistled. The shoes were practically new.

'The things people does throw away,' Eddoes said.

And he added, 'This is a helluva sort of job, you know. You could get anything if you really look. I know a man who get a whole bed the other day. And when I was picking up some rubbish from St Clair the other day this stupid woman rush out, begging me to come inside. She say she was going to give me a radio.'

Boyee said, 'You mean these rich people does just throw away things like that?'

Eddoes laughed and looked away, pitying our simplicity.

The news about Eddoes and the shoes travelled round the street pretty quickly. My mother was annoyed. She said, 'You see what sort of thing life is. Here I is, working my finger to the bone. Nobody flinging me a pair of shoes just like that, you know. And there you got that thin-arse little man, doing next to nothing, and look at all the things he does get.'

Eddoes presently began getting more things. He brought home a bedstead, he brought home dozens of cups and saucers only slightly cracked, lengths and lengths of wood, all sorts of bolts and screws, and sometimes even money.

Eddoes said, 'I was talking to one of the old boys today. He tell me the thing is to never throw away shoes. Always look in shoes people throw away, and you go find all sort of thing.'

The time came when we couldn't say if Eddoes was prouder of his job or of his collection of junk.

He spent half an hour a day unloading the junk from his cart.

And if anybody wanted a few nails, or a little piece of corrugated iron, the first person they asked was Eddoes.

He made a tremendous fuss when people asked him, though I feel he was pleased.

He would say, 'I working hard all day, getting all these materials and them, and people think they could just come running over and say, "Give me this, give me that."'

In time, the street referred to Eddoes's collection of junk as Eddoes's 'materials'.

One day, after he opened his school, Titus Hoyt was telling us that he had to spend a lot of money to buy books.

He said, 'It go cost me at least sixty dollars.'

Eddoes asked, 'How much book you getting for that?'

Titus Hoyt said, 'Oh, about seven or eight.'

Eddoes laughed in a scornful way.

Eddoes said, 'I could get a whole handful for you for about twelve cents. Why you want to go and spend so much money on eight books for?'

Eddoes sold a lot of books.

Hat bought twenty cents' worth of book.

It just shows how Titus Hoyt was making everybody educated.

And there was this business about pictures.

Eddoes said one day, 'Today, I pick up two nice pictures, two nice nice sceneries, done frame and everything.'

I went home and I said, 'Ma, Eddoes say he go sell us some sceneries for twelve cents.'

My mother behaved in an unexpected way.

She wiped her hand on her dress and came outside.

Eddoes brought the sceneries over. He said, 'The glass a little dirty, but you could always clean that. But they is nice sceneries.'

They were engravings of ships in stormy seas. I could see my mother almost ready to cry from joy. She repeated, 'I always always want to have some nice sceneries.' Then, pointing at me, she said to Eddoes, 'This boy father was always painting sceneries, you know.'

Eddoes looked properly impressed.

He asked, 'Sceneries nice as this?'

My mother didn't reply.

After a little talk my mother paid Eddoes ten cents.

And if Eddoes had something that nobody wanted to buy, he always went to my uncle Bhakcu, who was ready to buy anything.

He used to say, 'You never know when these things could come in handy.'

Hat began saying, 'I think all this materials getting on Eddoes' mind, you know. It have some men like that.'

I wasn't worried until Eddoes came to me one day and said, 'You ever think of collecting old bus-ticket?'

The idea had never crossed my mind.

Eddoes said, 'Look, there's something for a little boy like you to start with. For every thousand you collect I go give you a penny.'

I said, 'Why you want bus-ticket?' He laughed as though I were a fool.

I didn't collect any bus-tickets, but I noticed a lot of other boys doing so. Eddoes had told them that for every hundred they collected they got a free ride.

Hat said, 'Is to start getting worried when he begin collecting pins.'

*

But something happened that made Eddoes sober as a judge again.

He said one day, 'I in trouble!'

Hat said, 'Don't tell us that is thief you been thiefing all this materials and them?'

Eddoes shook his head.

He said, 'A girl making baby for me.'

Hat said, 'You sure is for you?'

Eddoes said, 'She say so.'

It was hard to see why this should get Eddoes so worried.

Hat said, 'But don't be stupid, man. Is the sort of thing that does happen to anybody.'

But Eddoes refused to be consoled.

He collected junk in a listless way.

Then he stopped altogether.

Hat said, 'Eddoes behaving as though he invent the idea of making baby.'

*

Hat asked again, 'You sure this baby is for you, and not for nobody else? It have some woman making a living this way, you know.'

Eddoes said, 'Is true she have other baby, but I in trouble.'

Hat said, 'She is like Laura?'

Eddoes said, 'Nah, Laura does only have one baby for one man. This girl does have two three.'

Hat said, 'Look, you mustn't worry. You don't know is your baby. Wait and see. Wait and see.'

Eddoes said sadly, 'She say if I don't take the baby she go make me lose my job.'

We gasped.

Eddoes said, 'She know lots of people. She say she go make them take me away from St Clair and put me in Dry River, where the people so damn poor they don't throw away nothing.'

I said, 'You mean you not going to find any materials there?'

Eddoes nodded, and we understood.

Hat said, 'The calypsonian was right, you hear.

Man centipede bad.
Woman centipede more than bad.

I know the sort of woman. She have a lot of baby, take the baby by the fathers, and get the fathers to pay money. By the time she thirty thirty-five, she getting so much money from so much man, and she ain't got no baby to look after and no responsibility. I know the thing.'

Boyee said, 'Don't worry, Eddoes. Wait and see if it is your baby. Wait and see.'

Hat said, 'Boyee, ain't you too damn small to be meddling with talk like this?'

*

The months dragged by.

One day Eddoes announced, 'She drop the baby yesterday.'

Hat said, 'Boy or girl?'

'Girl.'

We felt very sorry for Eddoes.

Hat asked, 'You think is yours?'

'Yes.'

'You bringing it home?'

'In about a year or so.'

'Then you ain't got nothing now to worry about. If is your child, bring she home, man. And you still going round St Clair, getting your materials.'

Eddoes agreed, but he didn't look any happier.

*

Hat gave the baby a nickname long before she arrived in Miguel Street. He called her Pleasure, and that was how she was called until she became a big girl.

The baby's mother brought Pleasure one night, but she didn't stay long. And Eddoes's stock rose when we saw how beautiful the mother was. She was a wild, Spanish-looking woman.

But one glance at Pleasure made us know that she couldn't be Eddoes's baby.

Boyee began whistling the calypso:

> Chinese children calling me Daddy!
> I black like jet,
> My wife like tar-baby,
> And still –
> Chinese children calling me Daddy!
> Oh God, somebody putting milk in my coffee.

Hat gave Boyee a pinch, and Hat said to Eddoes, 'She is a good-looking child, Eddoes. Like you.'

Eddoes said, 'You think so, Hat?'

Hat said, 'Yes, man. I think she go grow up to be a sweet girl just as how she father is a sweet-man.'

I said, 'You have a nice daughter, Eddoes.'

The baby was asleep and pink and beautiful.

Errol said, 'I could wait sixteen years until she come big enough.'

Eddoes by this time was smiling and for no reason at all was bursting out into laughter.

Hat said, 'Shut up, Eddoes. You go wake the baby up.'

And Eddoes asked, 'You really think she take after me, Hat?'

Hat said, 'Yes, man. I think you do right, you know, Eddoes. If I wasn't so careful myself and if I did have children outside I woulda bring them all home and put them down. Bring them all home and put them down, man. Nothing to shame about.'

Eddoes said, 'Hat, it have a bird-cage I pick up long time now. Tomorrow I go bring it for you.'

Hat said, 'Is a long long time now I want a good bird-cage.'

*

And in no time at all Eddoes became the old Eddoes we knew, proud of his job, his junk; and now proud, too, of Pleasure.

She became the street baby and all the women, Mrs Morgan, Mrs Bhakcu, Laura, and my mother, helped to look after her.

And if there was anyone in Miguel Street who wanted to laugh, he kept his mouth shut when Pleasure got the first prize in the Cow and Gate Baby competition, and her picture came out in the papers.

12. Love, Love, Love, Alone

ABOUT NINE O'CLOCK one morning a hearse and a motor-car stopped outside Miss Hilton's house. A man and a woman got out of the car. They were both middle-aged and dressed in black. While the man whispered to the two men in the hearse, the woman was crying in a controlled and respectable way.

So I suppose Miss Hilton got the swiftest and most private funeral in Miguel Street. It was nothing like the funeral we had for the other old widow, Miss Ricaud, the M.B.E. and social worker, who lived in a nicer part of the street. At that funeral I counted seventy-nine cars and a bicycle.

The man and the woman returned at midday and there was a bonfire in the yard. Mattresses and pillows and sheets and blankets were burned.

Then all the windows of the grey wooden house were thrown open, a thing I had never seen before.

At the end of the week a sign was nailed on the mango tree: FOR SALE.

Nobody in the street knew Miss Hilton. While she lived, her front gate was always padlocked and no one ever saw her leave or saw anybody go in. So even if you wanted to, you couldn't feel sorry and say that you missed Miss Hilton.

When I think of her house I see just two colours. Grey and green. The green of the mango tree, the grey of the house and the grey of the high galvanized-iron fence that prevented you from getting at the mangoes.

If your cricket ball fell in Miss Hilton's yard you never got it back.

It wasn't the mango season when Miss Hilton died. But we got back about ten or twelve of our cricket balls.

*

We were prepared to dislike the new people even before they came. I think we were a little worried. Already we had one man who kept on complaining about us to the police. He complained that we played cricket on the pavement; and if we weren't playing cricket he complained that we were making too much noise anyway.

Sergeant Charles would come and say, 'Boys, the Super send me. That blasted man ring up again. Take it a little easier.'

*

One afternoon when I came back from school Hat said, 'Is a man and a woman. She pretty pretty, but he ugly like hell, man. Portuguese, they look like.'

I didn't see much. The front gate was open, but the windows were shut again.

I heard a dog barking in an angry way.

One thing was settled pretty quickly. Whoever these people were they would never be the sort to ring up the police and say we were making noise and disturbing their sleep.

A lot of noise came from the house that night. The radio was going full blast until midnight when Trinidad Radio closed down. The dog was barking and the man was shouting. I didn't hear the woman.

There was a great peace next morning.

I waited until I saw the woman before going to school.

Boyee said, 'You know, Hat, I think I see that woman somewhere else. I see she when I was delivering milk up Mucurapo way.'

This lady didn't fit in with the rest of us in Miguel Street. She was too well-dressed. She was a little too pretty and a little too refined, and it was funny to see how she tried to jostle with the other women at Mary's shop trying to get scarce things like flour and rice.

I thought Boyee was right. It was easier to see this woman hopping about in shorts in the garden of one of the nice Mucurapo houses, with a uniformed servant fussing around in the background.

After the first few days I began to see more of the man. He was tall and thin. His face was ugly and had pink blotches.

Hat said, 'God, he is a first-class drinking-man, you hear.'

It took me some time to realize that the tall man was drunk practically all the time. He gave off a sickening smell of bad rum, and I was afraid of him. Whenever I saw him I crossed the road.

If his wife, or whoever she was, dressed better than any woman in the street, he dressed worse than any of us. He was even dirtier than George.

He never appeared to do any work.

I asked Hat, 'How a pretty nice woman like that come to get mix up with a man like that?'

Hat said, 'Boy, you wouldn't understand. If I tell you you wouldn't believe me.'

Then I saw the dog.

It looked as big as a ram-goat and as vicious as a bull. It had the same sort of thin face its master had. I used to see them together.

Hat said, 'If that dog ever get away it go have big trouble here in this street.'

A few days later Hat said, 'You know, it just strike me. I ain't see those people bring in any furnitures at all. It look like all they have is that radio.'

Eddoes said, 'It have a lot of things I could sell them.'

I used to think of the man and the dog and the woman in that house, and I felt sorry and afraid for the woman. I liked her too for the way she went about trying to make out that everything was all right for her, trying to make out that she was just another woman in the street, with nothing odd for people to notice.

Then the beatings began.

The woman used to run out screaming. We would hear the terrible dog barking and we would hear the man shouting and cursing and using language so coarse that we were all shocked.

Hat said to the bigger men, 'Is easy to put two and two and see what happening there.'

And Edward and Eddoes laughed.

I said, 'What happening, Hat?'

Hat laughed.

He said, 'You too small to know, boy. Wait until you in long pants.'

So I thought the worst.

The woman behaved as though she had suddenly lost all shame. She ran crying to anybody in the street, saying, 'Help me! Help me! He will kill me if he catches me.'

One day she rushed to our house.

She didn't make any apology for coming unexpectedly or anything like that. She was too wild and frightened even to cry.

I never saw my mother so anxious to help anyone. She gave the woman tea and biscuits. The woman said, 'I can't understand what has come over Toni these days. But it is only in the nights he is like this, you know. He is so kind in the mornings. But about midday something happens and he just goes mad.'

At first my mother was being excessively refined with the woman, bringing out all her fancy words and fancy pronunciations, pronouncing comfortable as cum-foughtable, and making war rhyme with bar, and promising that everything was deffy-nightly going to be all right. Normally my mother referred to males as man, but with this woman she began speaking about the ways of mens and them, citing my dead father as a typical example.

My mother said, 'The onliest thing with this boy father was that it was the other way round. Whenever I uses to go to the room where he was he uses to jump out of bed and run away bawling – run away screaming.'

But after the woman had come to us about three or four times my mother relapsed into her normal self, and began treating the woman as though she were like Laura or like Mrs Bhakcu.

My mother would say, 'Now, tell me, Mrs Hereira, why you don't leave this good-for-nothing man?'

Mrs Hereira said, 'It is a stupid thing to say to you or anybody else, but I like Toni. I love him.'

My mother said, 'Is a damn funny sort of love.'

Mrs Hereira began to speak about Toni as though he were a little boy she liked.

She said, 'He has many good qualities, you know. His heart is in the right place, really.'

My mother said, 'I wouldn't know about heart, but what I know is that he want a good clout on his backside to make him see sense. How you could let a man like that disgrace you so?'

Mrs Hereira said, 'No, I know Toni. I looked after him when he was sick. It is the war, you know. He was a sailor and they torpedoed him twice.'

My mother said, 'They shoulda try again.'

'You mustn't talk like this,' Mrs Hereira said.

My mother said, 'Look, I just talking my mind, you hear. You come here asking me advice.'

'I didn't ask for advice.'

'You come here asking me for help, and I just trying to help you. That's all.'

'I don't want your help or advice,' Mrs Hereira said.

My mother remained calm. She said, 'All right, then. Go back to the great man. Is my own fault, you hear. Meddling in white people business. You know what the calypso say:

> Is love, love, love, alone
> That cause King Edward to leave the throne.

Well, let me tell you. You not King Edward, you hear. Go back to your great love.'

Mrs Hereira would be out of the door, saying, 'I hope I never come back here again.'

But next evening she would be back.

One day my mother said, 'Mrs Hereira, everybody fraid that dog you have there. That thing too wild to be in a place like this.'

Mrs Hereira said, 'It isn't my dog. It's Toni's, and not even I can touch it.'

*

We despised Toni.

Hat said, 'Is a good thing for a man to beat his woman every now and then, but this man does do it like exercise, man.'

And he was also despised because he couldn't carry his liquor.

People used to find him sleeping in all sorts of places, dead drunk.

He made a few attempts to get friendly with us, making us feel uncomfortable more than anything else.

He used to say, 'Hello there, boys.'

And that appeared to be all the conversation he could make. And when Hat and the other big men tried to talk to him, as a kindness, I felt that Toni wasn't really listening.

He would get up and walk away from us suddenly, without a word, when somebody was in the middle of a sentence.

Hat said, 'Is a good thing too. I feel that if I look at him long enough I go vomit. You see what a dirty thing a white skin does be sometimes?'

And, in truth, he had a nasty skin. It was yellow and pink and white, with brown and black spots. The skin above his left eye had the raw pink look of scalded flesh.

But the strange thing I noticed was that if you just looked at Toni's hands and saw how thin and wrinkled they were, you felt sorry for him, not disgusted.

But I looked at his hands only when I was with Hat and the rest.

I suppose Mrs Hereira saw only his hands.

Hat said, 'I wonder how long this thing go last.'

*

Mrs Hereira obviously intended it to last a long time.

She and my mother became good friends after all, and I used to hear Mrs Heriera talking about her plans. She said one day she wanted some furniture, and I think she did get some in.

But most of the time she talked about Toni, and from the way she talked, anybody would believe that Toni was just an ordinary man.

She said, 'Toni is thinking about leaving Trinidad. We could start a hotel in Barbados.'

Or, 'As soon as Toni gets well again, we will go for a long cruise.'

And again, 'Toni is really a disciplined man, you know. Great will-power, really. We'll be all right when he gets his strength back.'

*

Toni still behaved as though he didn't know about all these plans for himself. He refused to settle down. He got wilder and more unpleasant.

[109]

Hat said, 'He behaving like some of those uncultured people from John-John. Like he forget that latrines make for some purpose.'

And that wasn't all. He appeared to develop an extraordinary dislike for the human race. One look at a perfect stranger was enough to start Toni cursing.

Hat said, 'We have to do something about Toni.'

I was there the evening they beat him up.

For a long time afterwards the beating-up was on Hat's mind.

It was a terrible thing, really. Hat and the rest of them were not angry. And Toni himself wasn't angry. He wasn't anything. He made no effort to return the blows. And the blows he got made no impression on him. He didn't look frightened. He didn't cry. He didn't plead. He just stood up and took it.

He wasn't being brave.

Hat said, 'He just too damn drunk.'

In the end Hat was angry with himself. He said, 'I taking advantage. We shouldnta do it. The man ain't have feelings, that's all.'

And from the way Mrs Hereira talked, it was clear that she didn't know what had happened.

Hat said, 'That's a relief, anyway.'

*

And through all these weeks, one question was always uppermost in our minds. How did a woman like Mrs Hereira get mixed up with Toni?'

Hat said he knew. But he wanted to know who Mrs Hereira was, and so did we all. Even my mother wondered aloud about this.

Boyee had an idea.

He said, 'Hat, you know the advertisements people does put out when their wife or their husband leave them?'

Hat said, 'Boyee, you know you getting too damn big too damn fast. How the hell a little boy like you know about a thing like that?'

Boyee took this as a compliment.

Hat said, 'How you know anyway that Mrs Hereira leave she husband? How you know that she ain't married to Toni?'

Boyee said, 'I telling you, Hat. I used to see that woman up Mucurapo way when I was delivering milk. I telling you so, man.'

Hat said, 'White people don't do that sort of thing, putting advertisement in the paper and thing like that.'

Eddoes said, 'You ain't know what you talking about, Hat. How much white people you know?'

In the end Hat promised to read the paper more carefully.

*

Then big trouble started.

Mrs Hereira ran out of her house screaming one day, 'He's going mad! He's going mad, I tell you. He will kill me this time sure.'

She told my mother, 'He grabbed a knife and began chasing me. He was saying, "I will kill you, I will kill you." Talking in a very quiet way.'

'You do him something?' my mother asked.

Mrs Hereira shook her head.

She said, 'It is the first time he threatened to kill me. And he was serious, I tell you.'

Up till then Mrs Hereira hadn't been crying, but now she broke down and cried like a girl.

She was saying, 'Toni has forgotten all I did for him. He has forgotten how I took care of him when he was sick. Tell me, you think that's right? I did everything for him. Everything. I gave up everything. Money and family. All for him. Tell me, is it right for him to treat me like this? Oh, God! What did I do to deserve all this?'

And so she wept and talked and wept.

We left her to herself for some time.

Then my mother said, 'Toni look like the sort of man who could kill easy, easy, without feeling that he really murdering. You want to sleep here tonight? You could sleep on the boy bed. He could sleep on the floor.'

Mrs Hereira wasn't listening.

My mother shook her and repeated her offer.

Mrs Hereira said, 'I am all right now, really. I will go back and talk to Toni. I think I did something to offend him. I must go back and find out what it is.'

'Well, I really give up,' my mother said. 'I think you taking this love business a little too far, you hear.'

So Mrs Hereira went back to her house. My mother and I waited for a long time, waiting for a scream.

But we heard nothing.

And the next morning Mrs Hereira was composed and refined as ever.

*

But day by day you could see her losing her freshness and saddening her beauty. Her face was getting lined. Her eyes were red and swollen, and the dark patches under them were ugly to look at.

*

Hat jumped up and said, 'I know it! I know it! I know it a long time now.'

He showed us the Personal column in the classified advertisements. Seven people had decided to leave their spouses. We followed Hat's finger and read:

> I, Henry Hubert Christiani, declare that my wife, Angela
> Mary Christiani, is no longer under my care and protection,
> and I am not responsible for any debt or debts contracted
> by her.

Boyee said, 'Is the selfsame woman.'

Eddoes said, 'Yes, Christiani. Doctor fellow. Know him good good. Used to pick rubbish for him.'

Hat said, 'Now I ask you, why, why a woman want to leave a man like that for this Toni?'

Eddoes said, 'Yes, know Christiani good good. Good house, nice car. Full of money, you know. It have a long time now I see him. Know him from the days when I used to work Mucurapo way.'

And in about half an hour the news had spread through Miguel Street.

*

My mother said to Mrs Hereira, 'You better call the police.'

Mrs Hereira said, 'No, no. Not the police.'

My mother said, 'Like you fraid police more than you fraid Toni.'

Mrs Hereira said, 'The scandal — '

'Scandal hell!' my mother said. 'You life in trouble and you thinking about scandal. Like if this man ain't disgrace you enough already.'

My mother said, 'Why you don't go back to your husband?'

She said it as though she expected Mrs Hereira to jump up in surprise.

But Mrs Hereira remained very calm.

She said, 'I don't feel anything about him. And I just can't stand that clean doctor's smell he has. It chokes me.'

I understood her perfectly, and tried to get my mother's eye.

Toni was growing really wild.

He used to sit on his front steps with a half-bottle of rum in his hand. The dog was with him.

He appeared to have lost touch with the world completely. He seemed to be without feeling. It was hard enough to imagine Mrs Hereira, or Mrs Christiani, in love with him. But it was impossible to imagine him being in love with anybody.

I thought he was like an animal, like his dog.

*

One morning, Mrs Hereira came over and said, very calmly, 'I have decided to leave Toni.'

She was so calm I could see my mother getting worried.

My mother said, 'What happen now?'

Mrs Hereira said, 'Nothing. Last night he made the dog jump at me. He didn't look as if he knew what he was doing. He didn't laugh or anything. I think he is going mad, and if I don't get out I think he will kill me.'

My mother said, 'Who you going back to?'

'My husband.'

'Even after what he print in the papers?'

Mrs Hereira said, 'Henry is like a boy, you know, and he thinks he can frighten me. If I go back today, he will be glad to have me back.'

And saying that, she looked different, and hard.

My mother said, 'Don't be so sure. He know Toni?'

Mrs Hereira laughed, in a crazy sort of way. 'Toni was Henry's friend, not mine. Henry brought him home one day. Toni was sick like anything. Henry was like that, you know. I never met a man who liked doing good works so much as Henry. He was all for good works and sanitation.'

My mother said, 'You know, Mrs Hereira, I really wish you was like me. If somebody did marry you off when you was fifteen, we wouldnta been hearing all this nonsense, you hear. Making all this damn fuss about your heart and love and all that rubbish.'

Mrs Hereira began to cry.

My mother said, 'Look, I didn't want to make you cry like this. I sorry.'

Mrs Hereira sobbed, 'No, it isn't you, it isn't you.'

My mother looked disappointed.

We watched Mrs Hereira cry.

Mrs Hereira said, 'I have left about a week's food with Toni.'

My mother said, 'Toni is a big man. You mustn't worry about him.'

*

He made terrible noises when he discovered that she had left him. He bayed like a dog and bawled like a baby.

Then he got drunk. Not drunk in the ordinary fashion; it got to the stage where the rum was keeping him going.

He forgot all about the dog, and it starved for days.

He stumbled drunk and crying from house to house, looking for Mrs Hereira.

And when he got back he took it out on the dog. We used to hear the dog yelping and growling.

In the end even the dog turned on him.

Somehow it managed to get itself free and it rushed at Toni.

Toni was shocked into sense.

The dog ran out of the house, and Toni ran after it. Toni squatted and whistled. The dog stopped, pricked up its ears, and turned round to look. It was funny seeing this drunk crazy man smiling and whistling at his dog, trying to get him back.

The dog stood still, staring at Toni.

Its tail wagged twice, then fell.

Toni got up and began walking towards the dog. The dog turned and ran.

*

We saw him sprawling on a mattress in one of the rooms. The room was perfectly empty. Nothing but the mattress and the empty rum bottles and the cigarette ends.

He was drunk and sleeping, and his face was strangely reposed. The thin and wrinkled hands looked so frail and sad.

*

Another FOR SALE sign was nailed to the mango tree. A man with about five little children bought the house.

From time to time Toni came around to terrify the new people.

He would ask for money, for rum, and he had the habit of asking for the radio. He would say, 'You have Angela's radio there. I charging rent for that, you know. Two dollars a month. Give me two dollars now.'

The new owner was a small man, and he was afraid of Toni. He never answered.

Toni would look at us and laugh and say, 'You know about Angela's radio, eh, boys? You know about the radio? Now, what this man playing at?'

Hat said, 'Who will tell me why they ever have people like Toni in this world!'

After two or three months he stopped coming to Miguel Street.

*

I saw Toni many years later.

I was travelling to Arima, and just near the quarry at Laventille I saw him driving a lorry.

He was smoking a cigarette.

That and his thin arms are all I remember.

And riding to Carenage one Sunday morning, I passed the Christiani's house, which I had avoided for a long time.

Mrs Christiani, or Mrs Hereira, was in shorts. She was reading the paper in an easy chair in the garden. Through the open doors of the house I saw a uniformed servant laying the table for lunch. There was a black car, a new, big car, in the garage.

13. The Mechanical Genius

My Uncle Bhakcu was very nearly a mechanical genius. I cannot remember a time when he was not the owner of a motor-vehicle of some sort. I don't think he always approved of the manufacturers' designs, however, for he was always pulling engines to bits. Titus Hoyt said that this was also a habit of the Eskimos. It was something he had got out of a geography book.

If I try to think of Bhakcu I never see his face. I can see only the soles of his feet as he worms his way under a car. I was worried when Bhakcu was under a car because it looked so easy for the car to slip off the jack and fall on him.

One day it did.

He gave a faint groan that reached the ears of only his wife.

She bawled, 'Oh God!' and burst into tears right away. 'I know something wrong. Something happen to *he*.'

Mrs Bhakcu always used this pronoun when she spoke of her husband.

She hurried to the side of the yard and heard Bhakcu groaning.

'Man,' she whispered, 'you all right?'

He groaned a little more loudly.

He said, 'How the hell I all right? You mean you so blind you ain't see the whole motor-car break up my arse?'

Mrs Bhakcu, dutiful wife, began to cry afresh.

She beat on the galvanized-iron fence.

'Hat,' Mrs Bhakcu called, 'Hat, come quick. A whole motor-car fall on *he*.'

Hat was cleaning out the cow-pen. When he heard Mrs Bhakcu he laughed. 'You know what I always does say,' Hat said. 'When you play the ass you bound to catch hell. The blasted car brand-new. What the hell he was tinkering with so?'

'*He* say the crank-shaft wasn't working nice.'

'And is there he looking for the crank-shaft?'

'Hat,' Bhakcu shouted from under the car, 'the moment you get this car from off me, I going to break up your tail.'

'Man,' Mrs Bhakcu said to her husband, 'how you so advantageous? The man come round with his good good mind to help you and now you want to beat him up?'

Hat began to look hurt and misunderstood.

Hat said, 'It ain't nothing new. Is just what I expect. Is just what I does always get for interfering in other people business. You know I mad to leave you and your husband here and go back to the cow-pen.'

'No, Hat. You mustn't mind *he*. Think what you would say if a whole big new motor-car fall on you.'

Hat said, 'All right, all right. I have to go and get some of the boys.'

We heard Hat shouting in the street. 'Boyee and Errol!'

No answer.

'Bo-yee and Ehhroll!'

'C-ming, Hat.'

'Where the hell you boys been, eh? You think you is man now and you could just stick your hands in your pocket and walk out like man? You was smoking, eh?'

'Smoking, Hat?'

'But what happen now? You turn deaf all of a sudden?'

'Was Boyee was smoking, Hat.'

'Is a lie, Hat. Was Errol really. I just stand up watching him.'

Miguel Street

'Somebody make you policeman now, eh? Is cut-arse for both of you. Errol, go cut a whip for Boyee. Boyee, go cut a whip for Errol.'

We heard the boys whimpering.

From under the car Bhakcu called, 'Hat, why you don't leave the boys alone? You go bless them bad one of these days, you know, and then they go lose you in jail. Why you don't leave the boys alone? They big now.'

Hat shouted back, 'You mind your own business, you hear. Otherwise I leave you under that car until you rotten, you hear.'

Mrs Bhakcu said to her husband, 'Take it easy, man.'

But it was nothing serious after all. The jack had slipped but the axle rested on a pile of wooden blocks, pinning Bhakcu to the ground without injuring him.

When Bhakcu came out he looked at his clothes. These were a pair of khaki trousers and a sleeveless vest, both black and stiff with engine grease.

Bhakcu said to his wife, 'They really dirty now, eh?'

She regarded her husband with pride. 'Yes, man,' she said. 'They really dirty.'

Bhakcu smiled.

Hat said, 'Look, I just sick of lifting up motor-car from off you, you hear. If you want my advice, you better send for a proper mechanic.'

Bhakcu wasn't listening.

He said to his wife, 'The crank-shaft was all right. Is something else.'

Mrs Bhakcu said, 'Well, you must eat first.'

She looked at Hat and said, '*He* don't eat when *he* working on the car unless I remind *he*.'

Hat said, 'What you want me do with that? Write it down with a pencil on a piece of paper and send it to the papers?'

I wanted to watch Bhakcu working on the car that evening,

so I said to him, 'Uncle Bhakcu, your clothes looking really dirty and greasy. I wonder how you could bear to wear them.'

He turned and smiled at me. 'What you expect, boy?' he said. 'Mechanic people like me ain't have time for clean clothes.'

'What happen to the car, Uncle Bhakcu?' I asked.

He didn't reply.

'The tappet knocking?' I suggested.

One thing Bhakcu had taught me about cars was that tappets were always knocking. Give Bhakcu any car in the world, and the first thing he would tell you about it was, 'The tappet knocking, you know. Hear. Hear it?'

'The tappet knocking?' I asked.

He came right up to me and asked eagerly, 'What, you hear it knocking?'

And before I had time to say, 'Well, something did knocking,' Mrs Bhakcu pulled him away, saying, 'Come and eat now, man. God, you get your clothes really dirty today.'

*

The car that fell on Bhakcu wasn't really a new car, although Bhakcu boasted that it very nearly was.

'It only do two hundred miles,' he used to say.

Hat said, 'Well, I know Trinidad small, but I didn't know it was so small.'

I remember the day it was bought. It was a Saturday. And that morning Mrs Bhakcu came to my mother and they talked about the cost of rice and flour and the black market. As she was leaving, Mrs Bhakcu said, '*He* gone to town today. He *say* he got to buy a new car.'

*

So we waited for the new car.

Midday came, but Bhakcu didn't.

Hat said, 'Two to one, that man taking down the engine right this minute.'

About four o'clock we heard a banging and a clattering, and looking down Miguel Street towards Docksite we saw the car. It was a blue Chevrolet, one of the 1939 models. It looked rich and new. We began to wave and cheer, and I saw Bhakcu waving his left hand.

We danced into the road in front of Bhakcu's house, waving and cheering.

The car came nearer and Hat said, 'Jump, boys! Run for your life. Like he get mad.'

It was a near thing. The car just raced past the house and we stopped cheering.

Hat said, 'The car out of control. It go have a accident, if something don't happen quick.'

Mrs Bhakcu laughed. 'What you think it is at all?' she said.

But we raced after the car, crying after Bhakcu.

He wasn't waving with his left hand. He was trying to warn people off.

By a miracle, it stopped just before Ariapita Avenue.

Bhakcu said, 'I did mashing down the brakes since I turn Miguel Street, but the brakes ain't working. Is a funny thing. I overhaul the brakes just this morning.'

Hat said, 'It have two things for you to do. Overhaul your head or haul your arse away before you get people in trouble.'

Bhakcu said, 'You boys go have to give me a hand to push the car back home.'

As we were pushing it past the house of Morgan, the pyro-technicist, Mrs Morgan shouted, 'Ah, Mrs Bhakcu, I see you buy a new car today, man.'

Mrs Bhakcu didn't reply.

Mrs Morgan said, 'Ah, Mrs Bhakcu, you think your husband go give me a ride in his new car?'

Mrs Bhakcu said, 'Yes, *he* go give you a ride, but first *your* husband must give *me* a ride on his donkey-cart when he buy it.'

Bhakcu said to Mrs Bhakcu, 'Why you don't shut your mouth up?'

Mrs Bhakcu said, 'But how you want me to shut my mouth up? You is my husband, and I have to stand up for you.'

Bhakcu said very sternly, 'You only stand up for me when I tell you, you hear.'

We left the car in front of Bhakcu's house, and we left Mr and Mrs Bhakcu to their quarrel. It wasn't a very interesting one. Mrs Bhakcu kept on claiming her right to stand up for her husband, and Mr Bhakcu kept on rejecting the claim. In the end Bhakcu had to beat his wife.

This wasn't as easy as it sounds. If you want to get a proper picture of Mrs Bhakcu you must consider a pear as a scale-model. Mrs Bhakcu had so much flesh, in fact, that when she held her arms at her sides, they looked like marks of parenthesis.

And as for her quarrelling voice . . .

Hat used to say, 'It sound as though it coming from a gramophone record turning fast fast backwards.'

For a long time I think Bhakcu experimented with rods for beating his wife, and I wouldn't swear that it wasn't Hat who suggested a cricket bat. But whoever suggested it, a second-hand cricket bat was bought from one of the groundsmen at the Queen's Park Oval, and oiled, and used on Mrs Bhakcu.

Hat said, 'Is the only thing she really could feel, I think.'

The strangest thing about this was that Mrs Bhakcu herself kept the bat clean and well-oiled. Boyee tried many times to borrow the bat, but Mrs Bhakcu never lent it.

*

So on the evening of the day when the car fell on Bhakcu I went to see him at work.

[123]

'What you did saying about the tappet knocking?' he said.

'I didn't say nothing,' I said. 'I was asking you.'

'Oh.'

Bhakcu worked late into the night, taking down the engine. He worked all the next day, Sunday, and all Sunday night. On Monday morning the mechanic came.

Mrs Bhakcu told my mother, 'The company send the mechanic man. The trouble with these Trinidad mechanics is that they is just piss-in-tail little boys who don't know the first thing about cars and things.'

I went round to Bhakcu's house and saw the mechanic with his head inside the bonnet. Bhakcu was sitting on the running-board, rubbing grease over everything the mechanic handed him. He looked so happy dipping his finger in the grease that I asked, 'Let me rub some grease, Uncle Bhakcu.'

'Go away, boy. You too small.'

I sat and watched him.

He said, 'The tappet was knocking, but I fix it.'

I said, 'Good.'

The mechanic was cursing.

I asked Bhakcu, 'How the points?'

He said, 'I have to check them up.'

I got up and walked around the car and sat on the running-board next to Bhakcu.

I looked at him and I said, 'You know something?'

'What?'

'When I did hear the engine on Saturday, I didn't think it was beating nice.'

Bhakcu said, 'You getting to be a real smart man, you know. You learning fast.'

I said, 'Is what you teach me.'

It was, as a matter of fact, pretty nearly the limit of my

knowledge. The knocking tappet, the points, the beat of the engine and – yes, I had forgotten one thing.

'You know, Uncle Bhakcu,' I said.

'What, boy?'

'Uncle Bhakcu, I think is the carburettor.'

'You really think so, boy?'

'I sure, Uncle Bhakcu.'

'Well, I go tell you, boy. Is the first thing I ask the mechanic. He don't think so.'

The mechanic lifted a dirty and angry face from the engine and said, 'When you have all sort of ignorant people messing about with a engine the white people build with their own hands, what the hell else you expect?'

Bhakcu winked at me.

He said, '*I* think is the carburettor.'

*

Of all the drills, I liked the carburettor drill the best. Sometimes Bhakcu raced the engine while I put my palm over the carburettor and off again. Bhakcu never told me why we did this and I never asked. Sometimes we had to siphon petrol from the tank, and I would pour this petrol into the carburettor while Bhakcu raced the engine. I often asked him to let me race the engine, but he wouldn't agree.

One day the engine caught fire, but I jumped away in time. The fire didn't last.

Bhakcu came out of the car and looked at the engine in a puzzled way. I thought he was annoyed with it, and I was prepared to see him dismantle it there and then.

That was the last time we did that drill with the carburettor.

*

At last the mechanic tested the engine and the brakes, and said, 'Look, the car good good now, you hear. It cost me more work than if I was to build over a new car. Leave the damn thing alone.'

After the mechanic left, Bhakcu and I walked very thoughtfully two or three times around the car. Bhakcu was stroking his chin, not talking to me.

Suddenly he jumped into the driver's seat, and pressed the horn-button a few times.

He said, 'What you think about the horn, boy?'

I said, 'Blow it again, let me hear.'

He pressed the button again.

Hat pushed his head through a window and shouted, 'Bhakcu, keep the damn car quiet, you hear, man. You making the place sound as though it have a wedding going on.'

We ignored Hat.

I said, 'Uncle Bhakcu, I don't think the horn blowing nice.'

He said, 'You really don't think so?'

I made a face and spat.

So we began to work on the horn.

When we were finished there was a bit of flex wound round the steering-column.

Bhakcu looked at me and said, 'You see, you could just take this wire now and touch it on any part of the metal-work, and the horn blow.'

It looked unlikely, but it did work.

I said, 'Uncle Bhakcu, how you know about all these things?'

He said, 'You just keep on learning all the time.'

*

The men in the street didn't like Bhakcu because they considered him a nuisance. But I liked him for the same reason that I liked Popo, the carpenter. For, thinking about it now, Bhakcu was also

The Mechanical Genius

an artist. He interfered with motor-cars for the joy of the thing, and he never seemed worried about money.

But his wife was worried. She, like my mother, thought that she was born to be a clever handler of money, born to make money sprout from nothing at all.

She talked over the matter with my mother one day.

My mother said, 'Taxi making a lot of money these days, taking Americans and their girl friends all over the place.'

So Mrs Bhakcu made her husband buy a lorry.

This lorry was really the pride of Miguel Street. It was a big new Bedford and we all turned out to welcome it when Bhakcu brought it home for the first time.

Even Hat was impressed. 'If is one thing the English people could build,' he said, 'is a lorry. This is not like your Ford and your Dodge, you know.'

Bhakcu began working on it that very afternoon, and Mrs Bhakcu went around telling people, 'Why not come and see how *he* working on the Bedford?'

From time to time Bhakcu would crawl out from under the lorry and polish the wings and the bonnet. Then he would crawl under the lorry again. But he didn't look happy.

The next day the people who had lent the money to buy the Bedford formed a deputation and came to Bhakcu's house, begging him to desist.

Bhakcu remained under the lorry all the time, refusing to reply. The money-lenders grew angry, and some of the women among them began to cry. Even that failed to move Bhakcu, and in the end the deputation just had to go away.

When the deputation left, Bhakcu began to take it out on his wife. He beat her and he said, 'Is you who want me to buy lorry. Is you. Is *you*. All you thinking about is money, money. Just like your mother.'

But the real reason for his temper was that he couldn't put

[127]

back the engine as he had found it. Two or three pieces remained outside and they puzzled him.

The agents sent a mechanic.

He looked at the lorry and asked Bhakcu, very calmly, 'Why you buy a Bedford?'

Bhakcu said, 'I like the Bedford.'

The mechanic shouted, 'Why the arse you didn't buy a Rolls-Royce? They does sell those with the engine sealed down.'

Then he went to work, saying sadly, 'Is enough to make you want to cry. A nice, new new lorry like this.'

The starter never worked again. And Bhakcu always had to use the crank.

Hat said, 'Is a blasted shame. Lorry looking new, smelling new, everything still shining, all sort of chalk-mark still on the chassis, and this man cranking it up like some old Ford pram.'

But Mrs Bhakcu boasted, 'Fust crank, the engine does start.'

One morning – it was a Saturday, market day – Mrs Bhakcu came crying to my mother. She said, '*He* in hospital.'

My mother said, 'Accident?'

Mrs Bhakcu said, '*He* was cranking up the lorry just outside the Market. Fust crank, the engine start. But it was in gear and it roll *he* up against another lorry.'

Bhakcu spent a week in hospital.

All the time he had the lorry, he hated his wife, and he beat her regularly with the cricket bat. But she was beating him too, with her tongue, and I think Bhakcu was really the loser in these quarrels.

It was hard to back the lorry into the yard and it was Mrs Bhakcu's duty and joy to direct her husband.

One day she said, 'All right, man, back back, turn a little to the right, all right, all clear. Oh God! No, no, no, man! Stop! You go knock the fence down.'

Bhakcu suddenly went mad. He reversed so fiercely he cracked the concrete fence. Then he shot forward again, ignoring Mrs Bhakcu's screams, and reversed again, knocking down the fence altogether.

He was in a great temper, and while his wife remained outside crying he went to his little room, stripped to his pants, flung himself belly down on the bed, and began reading the *Ramayana*.

The lorry wasn't making money. But to make any at all, Bhakcu had to have loaders. He got two of those big black Grenadian small-islanders who were just beginning to pour into Port of Spain. They called Bhakcu 'Boss' and Mrs Bhakcu 'Madam', and this was nice. But when I looked at these men sprawling happily in the back of the lorry in their ragged dusty clothes and their squashed-up felt hats, I used to wonder whether they knew how much worry they caused, and how uncertain their own position was.

Mrs Bhakcu's talk was now all about these two men.

She would tell my mother mournfully, 'Day after tomorrow we have to pay the loaders.' Two days later she would say, as though the world had come to an end, 'Today we pay the loaders.' And in no time at all she would be coming around to my mother in distress again, saying, 'Day after tomorrow we have to pay the loaders.'

Paying the loaders – for months I seemed to hear about nothing else. The words were well known in the street, and became an idiom.

Boyee would say to Errol on a Saturday, 'Come, let we go to the one-thirty show at Roxy.'

And Errol would turn out his pockets and say, 'I can't go, man. I pay the loaders.'

Hat said, 'It looks as though Bhakcu buy the lorry just to pay the loaders.'

The lorry went in the end. And the loaders too. I don't know what happened to them. Mrs Bhakcu had the lorry sold just at a time when lorries began making money. They bought a taxi. By now the competition was fierce and taxis were running eight miles for twelve cents, just enough to pay for oil and petrol.

Mrs Bhakcu told my mother, 'The taxi ain't making money.'

So she bought another taxi, and hired a man to drive it. She said, 'Two better than one.'

Bhakcu was reading the *Ramayana* more and more.

And even that began to annoy the people in the street.

Hat said, 'Hear the two of them now. She with that voice she got, and he singing that damn sing-song Hindu song.'

Picture then the following scene. Mrs Bhakcu, very short, very fat, standing at the pipe in her yard, and shrilling at her husband. He is in his pants, lying on his belly, dolefully intoning the *Ramayana*. Suddenly he springs up and snatches the cricket bat in the corner of the room. He runs outside and begins to beat Mrs Bhakcu with the bat.

The silence that follows lasts a few minutes.

And then only Bhakcu's voice is heard, as he does a solo from the *Ramayana*.

*

But don't think that Mrs Bhakcu lost any pride in her husband. Whenever you listened to the rows between Mrs Bhakcu and Mrs Morgan, you realized that Bhakcu was still his wife's lord and master.

Mrs Morgan would say, 'I hear your husband talking in his sleep last night, loud loud.'

'He wasn't talking,' Mrs Bhakcu said, 'he was singing.'

'Singing? Hahahahaaah! You know something, Mrs Bhakcu?'

'What, Mrs Morgan?'

'If your husband sing for his supper, both of all you starve like hell.'

'*He* know a damn lot more than any of the ignorant man it have in this street, you hear. *He* could read and write, you know.

English *and* Hindi. How you so ignorant you don't know that the *Ramayana* is a holy book? If you coulda understand all the good thing *he* singing, you wouldn't be talking all this nonsense you talking now, you hear.'

'How your husband this morning, anyway? He fix any new cars lately?'

'I not going to dirty my mouth arguing with you here, you hear. *He* know how to fix his car. Is a wonder nobody ain't tell your husband where he can fix all his so-call fireworks.'

*

Mrs Bhakcu used to boast that Bhakcu read the *Ramayana* two or three times a month. 'It have some parts he know by heart,' she said.

But that was little consolation, for money wasn't coming in. The man she had hired to drive the second taxi was playing the fool. She said, 'He robbing me like hell. He say that the taxi making so little money I owe him now.' She sacked the driver and sold the car.

She used all her financial flair. She began rearing hens. That failed because a lot of the hens were stolen, the rest attacked by street dogs, and Bhakcu hated the smell anyway. She began selling bananas and oranges, but she did that more for her own enjoyment than for the little money it brought in.

My mother said, 'Why Bhakcu don't go out and get a work?'

Mrs Bhakcu said, 'But how you want that?'

My mother said, '*I* don't want it. I was thinking about you.'

Mrs Bhakcu said, 'You could see he working with all the rude and crude people it have here in Port of Spain?'

My mother said, 'Well, he have to do something. People don't pay to see a man crawling under a motor-car or singing *Ramayana*.'

Mrs Bhakcu nodded and looked sad.

My mother said, 'But what I saying at all? You sure Bhakcu know the *Ramayana*?'

'I sure sure.'

My mother said, 'Well, it easy easy. He is a Brahmin, he know the *Ramayana*, and he have a car. Is easy for him to become a pundit, a real proper pundit.'

Mrs Bhakcu clapped her hands. 'Is a first-class idea. Hindu pundits making a lot of money these days.'

So Bhakcu became a pundit.

*

He still tinkered with his car. He had to stop beating Mrs Bhakcu with the cricket bat, but he was happy.

I was haunted by thoughts of the *dhoti*-clad Pundit Bhakcu, crawling under a car, attending to a crank-shaft, while poor Hindus waited for him to attend to their souls.

14. Caution

IT WAS NOT UNTIL 1947 that Bolo believed that the war was over. Up till then he used to say, 'Is only a lot of propaganda. Just lies for black people.'

In 1947 the Americans began pulling down their camp in the George V Park and many people were getting sad.

I went to see Bolo one Sunday and while he was cutting my hair he said, 'I hear the war over.'

I said, 'So I hear too. But I still have my doubts.'

Bolo said, 'I know what you mean. These people is master of propaganda, but the way I look at it is this. If they was still fighting they woulda want to keep the camp.'

'But they not keeping the camp,' I said.

Bolo said, 'Exactly. Put two and two together and what you get? Tell me, what you get?'

I said, 'Four.'

He clipped my hair thoughtfully for a few moments.

He said, 'Well, I glad the war over.'

When I paid for my trim I said, 'What you think we should do now, Mr Bolo? You think we should celebrate?'

He said, 'Gimme time, man. Gimme time. This is a big thing. I have to think it over.'

And there the matter rested.

*

I remember the night when the news of peace reached Port of Spain. People just went wild and there was a carnival in the streets. A new calypso sprang out of nothing and everybody was dancing in the streets to the tune of:

> All day and all night Miss Mary Ann
> Down by the river-side she taking man.

Bolo looked at the dancers and said, 'Stupidness! Stupidness! How black people so stupid?'

I said, 'But you ain't hear, Mr Bolo? The war over.'

He spat. 'How you know? You was fighting it?'

'But it come over on the radio and I read it in the papers.'

Bolo laughed. He said, 'Anybody would think you was still a little boy. You mean you come so big and you still does believe anything you read in the papers?'

I had heard this often before. Bolo was sixty and the only truth he had discovered seemed to be, 'You mustn't believe anything you read in the papers.'

It was his whole philosophy, and it didn't make him happy. He was the saddest man in the street.

I think Bolo was born sad. Certainly I never saw him laugh except in a sarcastic way, and I saw him at least once a week for eleven years. He was a tall man, not thin, with a face that was a caricature of sadness, the mouth curling downwards, the eyebrows curving downwards, the eyes big and empty of expression.

It was an amazement to me that Bolo made a living at all after he had stopped barbering. I suppose he would be described in a census as a carrier. His cart was the smallest thing of its kind I knew.

It was a little box on two wheels and he pushed it himself, pushed with his long body in such an attitude of resignation and futility you wondered why he pushed it at all. On this cart he could take just about two or three sacks of flour or sugar.

On Sundays Bolo became a barber again, and if he was proud of anything he was proud of his barbering.

Often Bolo said to me, 'You know Samuel?'

Samuel was the most successful barber in the district. He was so rich he took a week's holiday every year, and he liked everybody to know it.

I said, 'Yes, I know Samuel. But I don't like him to touch my hair at all. He can't cut hair. He does zog up my head.'

Bolo said, 'You know who teach Samuel all he know about cutting hair? You know?'

I shook my head.

'I. I teach Samuel. He couldn't even shave hisself when he start barbering. He come crying and begging, "Mr Bolo, Mr Bolo, teach me how to cut people hair, I beg you." Well, I teach him, and look what happen, eh. Samuel rich rich, and I still living in one room in this break-down old house. Samuel have a room where he does cut hair, I have to cut hair in the open under this mango tree.'

I said, 'But it nice outside, it better than sitting down in a hot room. But why you stop cutting hair regular, Mr Bolo?'

'Ha, boy, that is asking a big big question. The fact is, I just can't trust myself.'

'Is not true. You does cut hair good good, better than Samuel.'

'It ain't that I mean. Boy, when it have a man sitting down in front of you in a chair, and you don't like this man, and you have a razor in your hand, a lot of funny things could happen. I does only cut people hair these days when I like them. I can't cut any-and-everybody hair.'

*

Although in 1945 Bolo didn't believe that the war was over, in 1939 he was one of the great alarmists. In those days he bought all three Port of Spain newspapers, the *Trinidad Guardian*, the *Port of Spain Gazette*, and the *Evening News*. When the war broke out and the *Evening News* began issuing special bulletins, Bolo bought those too.

Those were the days when Bolo said, 'It have a lot of people who think they could kick people around. They think because we poor we don't know anything. But I ain't in that, you hear. Every day I sit down and read my papers regular regular.'

More particularly, Bolo was interested in the *Trinidad Guardian*. At one stage Bolo bought about twenty copies of that paper every day.

The *Guardian* was running a Missing Ball Competition. They printed a photograph of a football match in progress, but they had rubbed the ball out. All you had to do to win a lot of money was to mark the position of the ball with an X.

Spotting the missing ball became one of Bolo's passions.

In the early stages Bolo was happy enough to send in one X a week to the *Guardian*.

It was a weekly excitement for all of us.

Hat used to say, 'Bolo, I bet you forget all of us when you win the money. You leaving Miguel Street, man, and buying a big house in St Clair, eh?'

Bolo said, 'No, I don't want to stay in Trinidad. I think I go go to the States.'

Bolo began marking two X's. Then three, four, six. He never won a penny. He was getting almost constantly angry.

He would say, 'Is just a big bacchanal, you hear. The paper people done make up their mind long long time now who going to win the week prize. They only want to get all the black people money.'

Hat said, 'You mustn't get discouraged. You got try really hard again.'

Bolo bought sheets of squared paper and fitted them over the Missing Ball photograph. Wherever the lines crossed he marked an X. To do this properly Bolo had to buy something like a hundred to a hundred and fifty *Guardians* every week.

Sometimes Bolo would call Boyee and Errol and me and say, 'Now, boys, where you think this missing ball is? Look, I want you to shut your eyes and mark a spot with this pencil.'

And sometimes again Bolo would ask us, 'What sort of things you been dreaming this week?'

If you said you didn't dream at all, Bolo looked disappointed. I used to make up dreams and Bolo would work them out in relation to the missing ball.

People began calling Bolo 'Missing Ball'.

Hat used to say, 'Look the man with the missing ball.'

One day Bolo went up to the offices of the *Guardian* and beat up a sub-editor before the police could be called.

In court Bolo said, 'The ball not missing, you hear. It wasn't there in the first place.'

Bolo was fined twenty-five dollars.

The *Gazette* ran a story:

THE CASE OF THE MISSING BALL
Penalty for a foul

Altogether Bolo spent about three hundred dollars trying to spot the missing ball, and he didn't even get a consolation prize.

It was shortly after the court case that Bolo stopped barbering regularly and also stopped reading the *Guardian*.

I can't remember now why Bolo stopped reading the *Evening News*, but I know why he stopped reading the *Gazette*.

A great housing shortage arose in Port of Spain during the war, and in 1942 a philanthropist came to the rescue of the unhoused. He said he was starting a co-operative housing scheme. People who wished to take part in this venture had to deposit some two hundred dollars, and after a year or so they would get brand-new houses for next to nothing. Several important men blessed the new scheme, and lots of dinners were eaten to give the project a good start.

The project was heavily advertised and about five or six houses were built and handed over to some of the people who had eaten the dinners. The papers carried photographs of people putting keys into locks and stepping over thresholds.

Bolo saw the photographs and the advertisements in the *Gazette*, and he paid in his two hundred dollars.

In 1943 the Director of the Co-operative Housing Society disappeared and with him disappeared two or three thousand dream houses.

Bolo stopped reading the *Gazette*.

It was on a Sunday in November that year that Bolo made his announcement to those of us who were sitting under the mango tree, waiting for Bolo to cut our hair.

He said, 'I saying something now. And so help me God, if I ever break my word, it go be better if I lose my two eyes. Listen. I stop reading papers. If even I learn Chinese I ain't go read Chinese papers, you hearing. You mustn't believe anything you read in the papers.'

Bolo was cutting Hat's hair at the moment, and Hat hurriedly got up and left.

Later Hat said, 'You know what I think. We will have to stop getting trim from Bolo. The man get me really frighten now, you hear.'

We didn't have to think a lot about Hat's decision because a few days later Bolo came to us and said, 'I coming round to see you people one by one because is the last time you go see me.'

He looked so sad I thought he was going to cry.

Hat said, 'What you thinking of doing now?'

Bolo said, 'I leaving this island for good. Is only a lot of damn crooks here.'

Eddoes said, 'Bolo, you taking your box-cart with you?'

Bolo said, 'No. Why, you like it?'

Eddoes said, 'I was thinking. It look like good materials to me.'

Bolo said, 'Eddoes, take my box-cart.'

Hat said, 'Where you going, Bolo?'

Bolo said, 'You go hear.'

And so he left us that evening.

Eddoes said, 'You think Bolo going mad?'

Hat said, 'No. He going Venezuela. That is why he keeping so secret. The Venezuelan police don't like Trinidad people going over.'

Eddoes said, 'Bolo is a nice man and I sorry he leaving. You know, it have some people I know who go be glad to have that box-cart Bolo leave behind.'

We went to Bolo's little room that very evening and we cleaned it of all the useful stuff he had left behind. There wasn't much. A bit of oil-cloth, two or three old combs, a cutlass, and a bench. We were all sad.

Hat said, 'People really treat poor Bolo bad in this country. I don't blame him for leaving.'

Eddoes was looking over the room in a practical way. He said, 'But Bolo take away everything, man.'

Next afternoon Eddoes announced, 'You know how much I pick up for that box-cart? Two dollars!'

Hat said, 'You does work damn fast, you know, Eddoes.'

Then we saw Bolo himself walking down Miguel Street.

Hat said, 'Eddoes, you in trouble.'

Eddoes said, 'But he give it to me. I didn't thief it.'

Bolo looked tired and sadder than ever.

Hat said, 'What happen, Bolo? You make a record, man. Don't tell me you go to Venezuela and you come back already.'

Bolo said, 'Trinidad people! Trinidad people! I don't know why

Hitler don't come here and bomb all the sons of bitches it have in this island. He bombing the wrong people, you know.'

Hat said, 'Sit down, Bolo, and tell we what happen.'

Bolo said, 'Not yet. It have something I have to settle first. Eddoes, where my box-cart?'

Hat laughed.

Bolo said, 'You laughing, but I don't see the joke. Where my box-cart, Eddoes? You think you could make box-cart like that?'

Eddoes said, 'Your box-cart, Bolo? But you give it to me.'

Bolo said, 'I asking you to give it back to me.'

Eddoes said, 'I sell it, Bolo. Look the two dollars I get for it.'

Bolo said, 'But you quick, man.'

Eddoes was getting up.

Bolo said, 'Eddoes, it have one thing I begging you not to do. I begging you, Eddoes, not to come for trim by me again, you hear. I can't trust myself. And go and buy back my box-cart.'

Eddoes went away, muttering, 'Is a funny sort of world where people think their little box-cart so good. It like my big blue cart?'

Bolo said, 'When I get my hand on the good-for-nothing thief who take my money and say he taking me Venezuela, I go let him know something. You know what the man do? He drive around all night in the motor-launch and then put we down in a swamp, saying we reach Venezuela. I see some people. I begin talking to them in Spanish, they shake their head and laugh. You know is what? He put me down in Trinidad self, three four miles from La Brea.'

Hat said, 'Bolo, you don't know how lucky you is. Some of these people woulda kill you and throw you overboard, man. They say they don't like getting into trouble with the Venezuelan police. Is illegal going over to Venezuela, you know.'

We saw very little of Bolo after this. Eddoes managed to get the box-cart back, and he asked me to take it to Bolo.

Eddoes said, 'You see why black people can't get on in this

world. You was there when he give it to me with his own two hands, and now he want it back. Take it back to him and tell him Eddoes say he could go to hell.'

I told Bolo, 'Eddoes say he sorry and he send back the box-cart.'

Bolo said, 'You see how black people is. They only quick to take, take. They don't want to give. That is why black people never get on.'

I said, 'Mr Bolo, it have something I take too, but I bring it back. Is the oil-cloth. I did take it and give it to my mother, but she ask me to bring it back.'

Bolo said, 'Is all right. But, boy, who trimming you these days? You head look as though fowl sitting on it.'

I said, 'Is Samuel trim me, Mr Bolo. But I tell you he can't trim. You see how he zog up my head.'

Bolo said, 'Come Sunday, I go trim you.'

I hesitated.

Bolo said, 'You fraid? Don't be stupid. I like you.'

So I went on Sunday.

Bolo said, 'How you getting on with your lessons?'

I didn't want to boast.

Bolo said, 'It have something I want you to do for me. But I not sure whether I should ask you.'

I said, 'But ask me, Mr Bolo. I go do anything for you.'

He said, 'No, don't worry. I go tell you next time you come.'

A month later, I went again and Bolo said, 'You could read?'

I reassured him.

He said, 'Well, is a secret thing I doing. I don't want nobody to know. You could keep a secret?'

I said, 'Yes, I could keep a secret.'

'A old man like me ain't have much to live for,' Bolo said. 'A old man like me living by hisself have to have something to live for. Is why I doing this thing I tell you about.'

'What is this thing, Mr Bolo?'

He stopped clipping my hair and pulled out a printed sheet from his trouser pocket.

He said, 'You know what this is?'

I said, 'Is a sweepstake ticket.'

'Right. You smart, man. Is really a sweepstake ticket.'

I said, 'But what you want me do, Mr Bolo?'

He said, 'First you must promise not to tell anybody.'

I gave my word.

He said, 'I want you to find out if the number draw.'

The draw was made about six weeks later and I looked for Bolo's number. I told him, 'You number ain't draw, Mr Bolo.'

He said, 'Not even a proxime accessit?'

I shook my head.

But Bolo didn't look disappointed. 'Is just what I expect,' he said.

For nearly three years this was our secret. And all during those years Bolo bought sweepstake tickets, and never won. Nobody knew and even when Hat or somebody else said to him, 'Bolo, I know a thing you could try. Why you don't try sweepstake?' Bolo would say, 'I done with that sort of thing, man.'

At the Christmas meeting of 1948 Bolo's number was drawn. It wasn't much, just about three hundred dollars.

I ran to Bolo's room and said, 'Mr Bolo, the number draw.'

Bolo's reaction wasn't what I expected. He said, 'Look, boy, you in long pants now. But don't get me mad, or I go have to beat you bad.'

I said, 'But it really draw, Mr Bolo.'

He said, 'How the hell you know it draw?'

I said, 'I see it in the papers.'

At this Bolo got really angry and he seized me by the collar. He screamed, 'How often I have to tell you, you little good-for-nothing son of a bitch, that you mustn't believe all that you read in the papers?'

So I checked up with the Trinidad Turf Club.

I said to Bolo, 'Is really true.' Bolo refused to believe.

He said, 'These Trinidad people does only lie, lie. Lie is all they know. They could fool you, boy, but they can't fool me.'

I told the men of the street, 'Bolo mad like hell. The man win three hundred dollars and he don't want to believe.'

One day Boyee said to Bolo, 'Ay, Bolo, you win a sweepstake then.'

Bolo chased Boyee, shouting, 'You playing the ass, eh. You making joke with a man old enough to be your grandfather.'

And when Bolo saw me, he said, 'Is so you does keep secret? Is so you does keep secret? But why all you Trinidad people so, eh?'

And he pushed his box-cart down to Eddoes' house, saying, 'Eddoes, you want box-cart, eh? Here, take the box-cart.'

And he began hacking the cart to bits with his cutlass.

To me he shouted, 'People think they could fool me.'

And he took out the sweepstake ticket and tore it. He rushed up to me and forced the pieces into my shirt pocket.

*

Afterwards he lived to himself in his little room, seldom came out to the street, never spoke to anybody. Once a month he went to draw his old-age pension.

15. Until the Soldiers Came

EDWARD, HAT'S BROTHER, was a man of many parts, and I always thought it a sad thing that he drifted away from us. He used to help Hat with the cows when I first knew him and, like Hat, he looked settled and happy enough. He said he had given up women for good, and he concentrated on cricket, football, boxing, horse-racing, and cockfighting. In this way he was never bored, and he had no big ambition to make him unhappy.

Like Hat, Edward had a high regard for beauty. But Edward didn't collect birds of beautiful plumage, as Hat did. Edward painted.

His favourite subject was a brown hand clasping a black one. And when Edward painted a brown hand, it was a brown hand. No nonsense about light and shades. And the sea was a blue sea, and mountains were green.

Edward mounted his pictures himself and framed them in red passe-partout. The big department stores, Salvatori's, Fogarty's, and Johnson's, distributed Edward's work on commission.

To the street, however, Edward was something of a menace.

He would see Mrs Morgan wearing a new dress and say, 'Ah, Mrs Morgan, is a nice nice dress you wearing there, but I think it could do with some sort of decoration.'

Or he would see Eddoes wearing a new shirt and say, 'Eh, eh, Eddoes, you wearing a new shirt, man. You write your name in it, you know, otherwise somebody pick it up brisk brisk one of these days. Tell you what, I go write it for you.'

He ruined many garments in this way.

He also had the habit of giving away ties he had decorated himself. He would say, 'I have something for you. Take it and wear it. I giving it to you because I like you.'

And if the tie wasn't worn, Edward would get angry and begin shouting, 'But you see how ungrateful black people is. Listen to this. I see this man not wearing tie. I take a bus and I go to town. I walk to Johnson's and I look for the gents' department. I meet a girl and I buy a tie. I take a bus back home. I go inside my room and take up my brush and unscrew my paint. I dip my brush in paint and I put the brush on the tie. I spend two three hours doing that, and after all this, the man ain't wearing my tie.'

But Edward did a lot more than just paint.

One day, not many months after I had come to the street, Edward said, 'Coming back on the bus from Cocorite last night I only hearing the bus wheel cracking over crab back. You know the place by the coconut trees and the swamp? There it just crawling with crab. People say they even climbing up the coconut trees.'

Hat said, 'They does come out a lot at full moon. Let we go tonight and catch some of the crabs that Edward see.'

Edward said, 'Is just what I was going to say. We will have to take the boys because it have so much crab even they could pick up a lot.'

So we boys were invited.

Edward said, 'Hat, I was thinking. It go be a lot easier to catch the crab if we take a shovel. It have so much you could just shovel them up.'

Hat said, 'All right. We go take the cow-pen shovel.'

Edward said, 'That settle. But look, all-you have strong shoes? You better get strong shoes, you know, because these crab and them ain't playing big and if you don't look out they start walking away with your big toe before you know what is what.'

Hat said, 'I go use the leggings I does wear when I cleaning out the cow-pen.'

Edward said, 'And we better wear gloves. I know a man was catching crab one day and suddenly he see his right hand walking away from him. He look again and see four five crab carrying it away. This man jump up and begin one bawling. So we have to be careful. If you boys ain't have gloves just wrap some cloth over your hands. That go be all right.'

So late that night we all climbed into the Cocorite bus, Hat in his leggings, Edward in his, and the rest of us carrying cutlasses and big brown sacks.

The shovel Hat carried still stank from the cow-pen and people began squinging up their noses.

Hat said, 'Let them smell it. They does all want milk when the cow give it.'

People looked at the leggings and the cutlasses and the shovel and the sacks and looked away quickly. They stopped talking. The conductor didn't ask for our fares. The bus was silent until Edward began to talk.

Edward said, 'We must try and not use the cutlass. It ain't nice to kill. Try and get them live and put them in the bag.'

Many people got off at the next stop. By the time the bus got to Mucurapo Road it was carrying only us. The conductor stood right at the front talking to the driver.

Just before we got to the Cocorite terminus Edward said, 'Oh God, I know I was forgetting something. We can't bring back all the crab in a bus. I go have to go and telephone for a van.'

He got off one stop before the terminus.

We walked a little way in the bright moonlight, left the road and climbed down into the swamp. A tired wind blew from the sea, and the smell of stale sea-water was everywhere. Under the coconut trees it was dark. We walked a bit further in. A cloud covered the moon and the wind fell.

Hat called out, 'You boys all right? Be careful with your foot. I don't want any of you going home with only three toes.'

Boyee said, 'But I ain't seeing any crab.'

Ten minutes later Edward joined us.

He said, 'How many bags you full?'

Hat said, 'It look like a lot of people had the same idea and come and take away all the crab.'

Edward said, 'Rubbish. You don't see the moon ain't showing. We got to wait until the moon come out before the crab come out. Sit down, boys, let we wait.'

The moon remained clouded for half an hour.

Boyee said, 'It making cold and I want to go home. I don't think it have any crab.'

Errol said, 'Don't mind Boyee. I know him. He just frighten of the dark and he fraid the crab bite him.'

At this point we heard a rumbling in the distance.

Hat said, 'It look like the van come.'

Edward said, 'It ain't a van really. I order a big truck from Sam.'

We sat in silence waiting for the moon to clear. Then about a dozen torch-lights flashed all around us. Someone shouted, 'We ain't want any trouble. But if any one of you play the fool you going to get beat up bad.'

We saw what looked like a squad of policemen surrounding us.

Boyee began to cry.

Edward said, 'It have man beating their wife. It have people breaking into other people house. Why you policeman don't go and spend your time doing something with sense, eh? Just for a change.'

A policeman said, 'Why you don't shut up? You want me to spit in your mouth?'

Another policeman said, 'What you have in those bags?'

Edward said, 'Only crab. But take care. They is big crab and they go bite off your hand.'

Nobody looked inside the bags and then a man with a lot of stripes said, 'Everybody playing bad-man these days. Everybody getting full of smart answers, like the Americans and them.'

A policeman said, 'They have bag, they have cutlass, they have shovel, they have glove.'

Hat said, 'We was catching crab.'

The policeman said, 'With shovel? Eh, eh, what happen that you suddenly is God and make a new sort of crab you could catch with shovel?'

It took a lot of talk to make the policemen believe our story.

The officer in charge said, 'I go like to lay my hands on the son of a bitch who telephoned and say you was going to kill somebody.'

Then the policemen left.

It was late and we had missed the last bus.

Hat said, 'We had better wait for the truck Edward order.'

Edward said, 'Something tell me that truck ain't coming now.'

Hat said very slowly, half laughing and half serious, 'Edward, you is my own brother, but you know you really is a son of a bitch.'

Edward sat down and just laughed and laughed.

*

Then the war came. Hitler invaded France and the Americans invaded Trinidad. Lord Invader made a hit with his calypso:

> I was living with my decent and contented wife
> Until the soldiers came and broke up my life.

For the first time in Trinidad there was work for everybody, and the Americans paid well. Invader sang:

> Father, mother, and daughter
> Working for the Yankee dollar!
> Money in the land!
> The Yankee dollar, oh!

Edward stopped working in the cow-pen and got a job with the Americans at Chaguaramas.

Hat said, 'Edward, I think you foolish to do that. The Americans ain't here forever and ever. It ain't have no sense in going off and working for big money and then not having nothing to eat after three four years.'

Edward said, 'This war look as though it go last a long long time. And the Americans not like the British, you know. They does make you work hard, but they does pay for it.'

Edward sold his share of the cows to Hat, and that marked the beginning of his drift away from us.

Edward surrendered completely to the Americans. He began wearing clothes in the American style, he began chewing gum, and he tried to talk with an American accent. We didn't see much of him except on Sundays, and then he made us feel small and inferior. He grew fussy about his dress, and he began wearing a gold chain around his neck. He began wearing straps around his wrists, after the fashion of tennis-players. These straps were just becoming fashionable among smart young men in Port of Spain.

Edward didn't give up painting, but he no longer offered to paint things for us, and I think most people were relieved. He entered some poster competition, and when his design didn't win even a consolation prize, he grew really angry with Trinidad.

One Sunday he said, 'I was stupid to send in anything I paint with my own two hands for Trinidad people to judge. What they know about anything? Now, if I was in America, it woulda be different. The Americans is people. They know about things.'

To hear Edward talk, you felt that America was a gigantic

country inhabited by giants. They lived in enormous houses and they drove in the biggest cars of the world.

Edward used to say, 'Look at Miguel Street. In America you think they have streets so narrow? In America this street could pass for a sidewalk.'

One night I walked down with Edward to Docksite, the American army camp. Through the barbed wire you could see the huge screen of an open-air cinema.

Edward said, 'You see the sort of theatre they come and build in a stupid little place like Trinidad. Imagine the sort of thing they have in the States.'

And we walked down a little further until we came to a sentry in his box.

Edward used his best American accent and said, 'What's cooking, Joe?'

To my surprise the sentry, looking fierce under his helmet, replied, and in no time at all Edward and the sentry were talking away, each trying to use more swear-words than the other.

When Edward came back to Miguel Street he began swaggering along and he said to me, 'Tell them. Tell them how good I does get on with the Americans.'

And when he was with Hat he said, 'Was talking the other night with a American – damn good friend – and he was telling me that as soon as the Americans enter the war the war go end.'

Errol said, 'It ain't *that* we want to win the war. As soon as they make Lord Anthony Eden Prime Minister the war go end quick quick.'

Edward said, 'Shut up, kid.'

But the biggest change of all was the way Edward began talking of women. Up till then he used to say that he was finished with them for good. He made out that his heart had been broken a long time ago and he had made a vow. It was a vague and tragic story.

But now on Sundays Edward said, 'You should see the sort of

craft they have at the base. Nothing like these stupid Trinidad girls, you know. No, partner. Girls with style, girls with real class.'

I think it was Eddoes who said, 'I shouldn't let it worry you. They wouldn't tangle with you, those girls. They want big big American men. You safe.'

Edward called Eddoes a shrimp and walked away in a huff.

He began lifting weights, and in this, too, Edward was running right at the head of fashion. I don't know what happened in Trinidad about that time, but every young man became suddenly obsessed with the Body Beautiful idea, and there were physique competitions practically every month. Hat used to console himself by saying, 'Don't worry. Is just a lot of old flash, you hear. They say they building muscle muscle. Just let them cool off and see what happen. All that thing they call muscle turn fat, you know.'

Eddoes said, 'Is the funniest sight you could see. At the Dairies in Philip Street all you seeing these days is a long line of black black men sitting at the counter and drinking quart bottles of white milk. All of them wearing sleeveless jersey to show off their big arm.'

In about three months Edward made his appearance among us in a sleeveless jersey. He had become a really big man.

Presently he began talking about the women at the base who were chasing him.

He said, 'I don't know what they see in me.'

*

Somebody had the idea of organizing a Local Talent on Parade show and Edward said, 'Don't make me laugh. What sort of talent they think Trinidad have?'

The first show was broadcast and we all listened to it in Eddoes' house, Edward kept on laughing all the time.

Hat said, 'Why you don't try singing yourself, then?'

Edward said, 'Sing for who? Trinidad people?'

Hat said, 'Do them a favour.'

To everybody's surprise Edward began singing, and the time came when Hat had to say, 'I just can't live in the same house with Edward. I think he go have to move.'

Edward moved, but he didn't move very far. He remained on our side of Miguel Street.

He said, 'Is a good thing. I was getting tired of the cow smell.'

Edward went up for one of the Local Talent shows and in spite of everything we all hoped that he would win a prize of some sort. The show was sponsored by a biscuit company and I think the winner got some money.

'They does give the others a thirty-one-cent pack of biscuits,' Hat said.

Edward got a package of biscuits.

He didn't bring it home, though. He threw it away.

He said, 'Throw it away. Why I shouldn't throw it away? You see, is just what I does tell you. Trinidad people don't know good thing. They just born stupid. Down at the base it have Americans *begging* me to sing. They know what is what. The other day, working and singing at the base, the colonel come up and tell me I had a nice voice. He was begging me to go to the States.'

Hat said, 'Why you don't go then?'

Edward said fiercely, 'Gimme time. Wait and see if I don't go.'

Eddoes said, 'What about all those woman and them who was chasing you? They catch up with you yet or they pass you?'

Edward said, 'Listen, Joe, I don't want to start getting tough with you. Do me a favour and shut up.'

When Edward brought any American friends to his house he pretended that he didn't know us, and it was funny to see him walking with them, holding his arms in the American way, hanging loosely, like a gorilla's.

Hat said, 'All the money he making he spending it on rum and ginger, curryfavouring with them Americans.'

In a way, I suppose, we were all jealous of him.

Hat began saying, 'It ain't hard to get a work with the Americans. I just don't want to have boss, that's all. I like being my own boss.'

Edward didn't mix much with us now.

*

One day he came to us with a sad face and said, 'Hat, it look like if I have to get married.'

He spoke with his Trinidad accent.

Hat looked worried. He said, 'Why? Why? Why you have to get married?'

'She making baby.'

'Is a damn funny thing to say. If everybody married because woman making baby for them it go be a hell of a thing. What happen that you want to be different now from everybody else in Trinidad? You come so American?'

Edward hitched up his tight American-style trousers and made a face like an American film actor. He said, 'You know all the answers, don't you? This girl is different. Sure I fall in love maybe once maybe twice before, but this kid's different.'

Hat said, 'She's got what it takes?'

Edward said, 'Yes.'

Hat said, 'Edward, you is a big man. It clear that you make up your mind to married this girl. Why you come round trying to make me force you to married her? You is a big man. You ain't have to come to me to get permission to do this to do that.'

When Edward left, Hat said, 'Whenever Edward come to me with a lie, he like a little boy. He can't lie to me. But if he married this girl, although I ain't see she, I feel he go live to regret it.'

*

Edward's wife was a tall and thin white-skinned woman. She looked very pale and perpetually unwell. She moved as though every step cost her effort. Edward made a great fuss about her and never introduced us.

The women of the street lost no time in passing judgement.

Mrs Morgan said, 'She is a born trouble-maker, that woman. I feel sorry for Edward. He got hisself in one mess.'

Mrs Bhakcu said, 'She is one of these modern girls. They want their husband to work all day and come home and cook and wash and clean up. All they know is to put powder and rouge on their face and walk out swinging their backside.'

And Hat said, 'But how she making baby? I can't see anything.'

Edward dropped out of our circle completely.

Hat said, 'She giving him good hell.'

And one day, Hat shouted across the road to Edward, 'Joe, come across here for a moment.'

Edward looked very surly. He asked in Trinidadian, 'What you want?'

Hat smiled and said, 'What about the baby? When it coming?'

Edward said, 'What the hell you want to know for?'

Hat said, 'I go be a funny sort of uncle if I wasn't interested in my nephew.'

Edward said, 'She ain't making no more baby.'

Eddoes said, 'So it was just a line she was shooting then?'

Hat said, 'Edward, you lying. You make up all that in the first place. She wasn't making no baby, and you know that. She didn't tell you she was making baby, and you know that too. If you want to married the woman why you making all this thing about it?'

Edward looked very sad. 'If you want to know the truth, I don't think she could make baby.'

And when this news filtered through to the women of the street, they all said what my mother said.

She said, 'How you could see pink and pale people ever making baby?'

And although we had no evidence, and although Edward's house was still noisy with Americans, we felt that all was not well with Edward and his wife.

*

One Friday, just as it was getting dark, Edward ran up to me and said, 'Put down that stupidness you reading and go and get a policeman.'

I said, 'Policeman? But how I go go and get policeman just like that.'

Edward said, 'You could ride?'

I said, 'Yes.'

Edward said, 'You have a bicycle lamp?'

I said, 'No.'

Edward said, 'Take the bike and ride without lamp. You bound to get policeman.'

I said, 'And when I get this policeman, what I go tell him?'

Edward said, 'She try to kill sheself again.'

Before I had cycled to Ariapita Avenue I had met not one but two policemen. One of them was a sergeant. He said, 'You thinking of going far, eh?'

I said, 'Is you I was coming to find.'

The other policeman laughed.

The sergeant said to him, 'He smart, eh? I feel the magistrate go like that excuse. Is a new one and even me like it.'

I said, 'Come quick, Edward wife try to kill sheself again.'

The sergeant said, 'Oh, Edward wife always killing sheself, eh?' And he laughed. He added, 'And where this Edward wife try to kill sheself again, eh?'

I said, 'Just a little bit down Miguel Street.'

The constable said, 'He really smart, you know.'

The sergeant said, 'Yes. We leave him here and go and find somebody who try to kill sheself. Cut out this nonsense, boy. Where your bicycle licence?'

I said, 'Is true what I telling you. I go come back with you and show you the house.'

Edward was waiting for us. He said, 'You take a damn long time getting just two policemen.'

The policemen went inside the house with Edward and a little crowd gathered on the pavement.

Mrs Bhakcu said, 'Is just what I expect. I know from the first it was going to end up like this.'

Mrs Morgan said, 'Life is a funny thing. I wish I was like she and couldn't make baby. And it have a woman now trying to kill sheself because she can't make baby.'

Eddoes said, 'How you know is that she want to kill sheself for?'

Mrs Morgan shook a fat shoulder. 'What else?'

From then on I began to feel sorry for Edward because the men in the street and the women didn't give him a chance. And no matter how many big parties Edward gave at his house for Americans, I could see that he was affected when Eddoes shouted, 'Why you don't take your wife to America, boy? Those American doctors smart like hell, you know. They could do anything.' Or when Mrs Bhakcu suggested that she should have a blood test at the Caribbean Medical Commission at the end of Ariapita Avenue.

The parties at Edward's house grew wilder and more extravagant. Hat said, 'Every party does have an end and have to go home. Edward only making hisself more miserable.'

The parties certainly were not making Edward's wife any happier. She still looked frail and cantankerous, and now we sometimes heard Edward's voice raised in argument with her. It was not the usual sort of man-and-wife argument we had in the street. Edward sounded exasperated, but anxious to please.

Eddoes said, 'I wish any woman I married try behaving like that. Man, I give she one good beating and I make she straight straight like bamboo.'

Hat said, 'Edward ask for what he get. And the stupid thing is that I believe Edward really love the woman.'

Edward would talk to Hat and Eddoes and the other big men when they spoke to him, but when we boys tried talking to him, he had no patience. He would threaten to beat us and so we left him alone.

But whenever Edward passed, Boyee, brave and stupid as ever, would say in an American accent, 'What's up, Joe?'

Edward would stop and look angrily at Boyee and then lunge at him, shouting and swearing. He used to say, 'You see the sort of way Trinidad children does behave? What else this boy want but a good cut-arse?'

One day Edward caught Boyee and began flogging him.

At every stroke Boyee shouted, 'No, Edward.'

And Edward got madder and madder.

Then Hat ran up and said, 'Edward, put down that boy this minute or else it have big big trouble in this street. Put him down, I tell you. I ain't fraid of your big arms, you know.'

The men in the street had to break up the fight.

And when Boyee was freed, he shouted to Edward, 'Why you don't make child yourself and then beat it?'

Hat said, 'Boyee, I going to cut your tail this minute. Errol, go break a good whip for me.'

*

It was Edward himself who broke the news.

He said, 'She leave me.' He spoke in a very casual way.

Eddoes said, 'I sorry too bad, Edward.'

Hat said, 'Edward, boy, the things that not to be don't be.'

Edward didn't seem to be paying too much attention.

So Eddoes went on, 'I didn't like she from the first and I don't think a man should married a woman who can't make baby – '

Edward said, 'Eddoes, shut your thin little mouth up. And you, too, Hat, giving me all this make-up sympathy. I know how sad all-you is, all-you so sad all-you laughing.'

Hat said, 'But who laughing? Look, Edward, go and give anybody else all this temper, you hear, but leave me out. After all, it ain't nothing strange for a man wife to run away. Is like the calypso Invader sing:

> I was living with my decent and contented wife
> Until the soldiers came and broke up my life.

It ain't your fault, is the Americans' fault.'

Eddoes said, 'You know who she run away with?'

Edward said, 'You hear me say she run away with anybody?'

Eddoes said, 'No, you didn't say that, but is what I feel.'

Edward said sadly, 'Yes, she run away. With a American soldier. And I give the man so much of my rum to drink.'

But after a few days Edward was running around telling people what had happened and saying, 'Is a damn good thing. I don't want a wife that can't make baby.'

And now nobody made fun of Edward's Americanism, and I think we were all ready to welcome him back to us. But he wasn't really interested. We hardly saw him in the street. When he wasn't working he was out on some excursion.

Hat said, 'Is love he really love she. He looking for she.'

In the calypso by Lord Invader the singer loses his wife to the Americans and when he begs her to come back to him, she says:

> 'Invader, I change my mind,
> I living with my Yankee soldier.'

This was exactly what happened to Edward.

He came back in a great temper. He was miserable. He said, 'I leaving Trinidad.'

Eddoes said, 'Where you going? America?'

Edward almost cuffed Eddoes.

Hat said, 'But how you want to let one woman break up your life so? You behaving as if you is the first man this thing happen to.'

But Edward didn't listen.

At the end of the month he sold his house and left Trinidad. I think he went to Aruba or Curaçao, working with the big Dutch oil company.

*

And some months later Hat said, 'You know what I hear? Edward wife have a baby for she American.'

16. Hat

HAT LOVED TO make a mystery of the smallest things. His relationship to Boyee and Errol, for instance. He told strangers they were illegitimate children of his. Sometimes he said he wasn't sure whether they were his at all, and he would spin a fantastic story about some woman both he and Edward lived with at the same time. Sometimes again, he would make out that they were his sons by an early marriage, and you felt you could cry when you heard Hat tell how the boys' mother had gathered them around her death-bed and made them promise to be good.

It took me some time to find out that Boyee and Errol were really Hat's nephews. Their mother, who lived up in the bush near Sangre Grande, died soon after her husband died, and the boys came to live with Hat.

The boys showed Hat little respect. They never called him Uncle, only Hat; and for their part they didn't mind when Hat said they were illegitimate. They were, in fact, willing to support any story Hat told about their birth.

I first got to know Hat when he offered to take me to the cricket at the Oval. I soon found out that he had picked up eleven other boys from four or five streets around, and was taking them as well.

We lined up at the ticket-office and Hat counted us loudly. He said, 'One and twelve half.'

Many people stopped minding their business and looked up.

The man selling tickets said, 'Twelve half?'

Hat looked down at his shoes and said, 'Twelve half.'

We created a lot of excitement when all thirteen of us, Hat at the head, filed around the ground, looking for a place to sit.

People shouted, 'They is all yours, mister?'

Hat smiled, weakly, and made people believe it was so. When we sat down he made a point of counting us loudly again. He said, 'I don't want your mother raising hell when I get home, saying one missing.'

It was the last day of the last match between Trinidad and Jamaica. Gerry Gomez and Len Harbin were making a great stand for Trinidad, and when Gomez reached his 150 Hat went crazy and danced up and down, shouting, 'White people is God, you hear!'

A woman selling soft drinks passed in front of us.

Hat said, 'How you selling this thing you have in the glass and them?'

The woman said, 'Six cents a glass.'

Hat said, 'I want the wholesale price. I want thirteen.'

The woman said, 'These children is all yours?'

Hat said, 'What wrong with that?'

The woman sold the drinks at five cents a glass.

When Len Harbin was 89, he was out lbw, and Trinidad declared.

Hat was angry. 'Lbw? Lbw? How he lbw? Is only a lot of robbery. And is a Trinidad umpire too. God, even umpires taking bribe now.'

Hat taught me many things that afternoon. From the way he pronounced them, I learned about the beauty of cricketers' names, and he gave me all his own excitement at watching a cricket match.

I asked him to explain the scoreboard.

He said, 'On the left-hand side they have the names of the batsman who finish batting.'

I remember that because I thought it such a nice way of saying that a batsman was out: to say that he had finished batting.

All during the tea interval Hat was as excited as ever. He tried to get all sorts of people to take all sorts of crazy bets. He ran about waving a dollar-note and shouting, 'A dollar to a shilling, Headley don't reach double figures.' Or, 'A dollar, Stollmeyer field the first ball.'

The umpires were walking out when one of the boys began crying.

Hat said, 'What you crying for?'

The boy cried and mumbled.

Hat said, 'But what you crying for?'

A man shouted, 'He want a bottle.'

Hat turned to the man and said, 'Two dollars, five Jamaican wickets fall this afternoon.'

The man said, 'Is all right by me, if is hurry you is to lose your money.'

A third man held the stakes.

The boy was still crying.

Hat said, 'But you see how you shaming me in front of all these people? Tell me quick what you want.'

The boy only cried. Another boy came up to Hat and whispered in his ear.

Hat said, 'Oh, God! How? Just when they coming out.'

He made us all stand. He marched us away from the grounds and made us line up against the galvanized-iron paling of the Oval.

He said, 'All right, now, pee. Pee quick, all of all-you.'

The cricket that afternoon was fantastic. The Jamaican team, which included the great Headley, lost six wickets for thirty-one runs. In the fading light the Trinidad fast bowler, Tyrell Johnson, was unplayable, and his success seemed to increase his speed.

A fat old woman on our left began screaming at Tyrell Johnson, and whenever she stopped screaming she turned to us and said very quietly, 'I know Tyrell since he was a boy so high. We use to pitch marble together.' Then she turned away and began screaming again.

Hat collected his bet.

This, I discovered presently, was one of Hat's weaknesses – his passion for impossible bets. At the races particularly, he lost a lot of money, but sometimes he won, and then he made so much he could afford to treat all of us in Miguel Street.

I never knew a man who enjoyed life as much as Hat did. He did nothing new or spectacular – in fact, he did practically the same things every day – but he always enjoyed what he did. And every now and then he managed to give a fantastic twist to some very ordinary thing.

He was a bit like his dog. This was the tamest Alsatian I have ever known. One of the things I noticed in Miguel Street was the way dogs resembled their owners. George had a surly, mean mongrel. Tom's dog was a terrible savage. Hat's dog was the only Alsatian I knew with a sense of humour.

In the first place it behaved oddly, for an Alsatian. You could make it the happiest dog on earth if you flung things for it to retrieve. One day, in the Savannah, I flung a guava, into some thick bushes. He couldn't get at the guava, and he whined and complained. He suddenly turned and ran back past me, barking loudly. While I turned to see what was wrong, he ran back to the bushes. I saw nothing strange, and when I looked back I was just in time to see him taking another guava behind the bushes.

I called him and he rushed up whining and barking.

I said, 'Go on, boy. Go on and get the guava.'

He ran back to the bushes and poked and sniffed a bit and then dashed behind the bushes to get the guava he had himself placed there.

I only wish the beautiful birds Hat collected were as tame as the Alsatian. The macaws and the parrots looked like angry and quarrelsome old women and they attacked anybody. Sometimes Hat's house became a dangerous place with all these birds around. You would be talking quietly when you would suddenly feel a prick and a tug on your calf. The macaw or the parrot. Hat tried to make us believe they didn't bite him, but I know that they did.

Strange that both Hat and Edward became dangerous when they tried meddling with beauty. There was Edward with his painting, and Hat with his sharp-beaked macaws.

Hat was always getting into trouble with the police. Nothing serious, though. A little cockfighting here, some gambling there, a little drinking somewhere else, and so on.

But it never soured him against the law. In fact, every Christmas Sergeant Charles, with the postman and the sanitary inspector, came to Hat's place for a drink.

Sergeant Charles would say, 'Is only a living I have to make, you know, Hat. Nobody ain't have to tell me. I know I ain't going to get any more promotion, but still.'

Hat would say, 'Is all right, Sergeant. None of we don't mind. How your children these days? How Elijah?'

Elijah was a bright boy.

'Elijah? Oh, I think he go get a exhibition this year. Is all we could do, eh, Hat? All we could do is try. We can't do no more.'

And they always separated as good friends.

But once Hat got into serious trouble for watering his milk.

He said, 'The police and them come round asking me how the water get in the milk. As if I know. I ain't know how the water get there. You know I does put the pan in water to keep the milk cool, and prevent it from turning. I suppose the pan did have a hole, that's all. A tiny little hole.'

Edward said, 'It better to be frank and tell the magistrate that.'

Hat said, 'Edward, you talking as if Trinidad is England. You ever hear that people tell the truth in Trinidad and get away? In Trinidad the more you innocent, the more they throw you in jail, and the more bribe you got to hand out. You got to bribe the magistrate. You got to give them fowl, big Leghorn hen, and you got to give them money. You got to bribe the inspectors. By the time you finish bribing it would be better if you did take your jail quiet quiet.'

Edward said, 'It is the truth. But you can't plead guilty. You have to make up some new story.'

Hat was fined two hundred dollars and the magistrate preached a long sermon at him.

He was in a real temper when he came back from court. He tore off his tie and coat and said, 'Is a damn funny world. You bathe, you put on a clean shirt, you put on tie and you put on jacket, you shine up your shoe. And all for what? Is only to go in front of some stupid magistrate for him to abuse you.'

It rankled for days.

Hat said, 'Hitler was right, man. Burn all the law books. Burn all of them up. Make a big pile and set fire to the whole damn thing. Burn them up and watch them burn. Hitler was right, man. I don't know why we fighting him for.'

Eddoes said, 'You talking a lot of nonsense, you know, Hat.'

Hat said, 'I don't want to talk about it. Don't want to talk about it. Hitler was right. Burn the law books. Burn all of them up. Don't want to talk about it.'

For three months Hat and Sergeant Charles were not on speaking terms. Sergeant Charles was hurt, and he was always sending messages of goodwill to Hat.

One day he called me and said, 'You go be seeing Hat this evening?'

I said, 'Yes.'

'You did see him yesterday?'

'Yes.'

'How he is?'

'How?'

'Well, I mean, how he looking? He looking well? Happy?'

I said, 'He looking damn vex.'

Sergeant Charles said, 'Oh.'

I said, 'All right.'

'Look, before you go away – '

'What?'

'Nothing. No, no. Wait before you go. Tell Hat how for me, you hear.'

I told Hat, 'Sergeant Charles call me to his house today and begin one crying and begging. He keep on asking me to tell you that he not vex with you, that it wasn't he who tell the police about the milk and the water.'

Hat said, '*Which* water in *which* milk?'

I didn't know what to say.

Hat said, 'You see the sort of place Trinidad coming now. Somebody say it had water in my milk. Nobody see me put water in the milk, but everybody talking now as if they see me. Everybody talking about *the* water in *the* milk.'

Hat, I saw, was enjoying even this.

*

I always looked upon Hat as a man of settled habits, and it was hard to think of him looking otherwise than he did. I suppose he was thirty-five when he took me to that cricket-match, and forty-three when he went to jail. Yet he always looked the same to me.

In appearance, as I have said, he was like Rex Harrison. He was dark-brown in complexion, of medium height medium build. He had a slightly bow-legged walk and he had flat feet.

I was prepared to see him do the same things for the rest of his life. Cricket, football, horse-racing; read the paper in the mornings and afternoons; sit on the pavement and talk; get noisily drunk on Christmas Eve and New Year's Eve.

He didn't appear to need anything else. He was self-sufficient, and I didn't believe he even needed women. I knew, of course, that he visited certain places in the city from time to time, but I thought he did this more for the vicious thrill than for the women.

And then this thing happened. It broke up the Miguel Street Club, and Hat himself was never the same afterwards.

In a way, I suppose, it was Edward's fault. I don't think any of us realized how much Hat loved Edward and how heartbroken he was when Edward got married. He couldn't hide his delight when Edward's wife ran away with the American soldier, and he was greatly disappointed when Edward went to Aruba.

Once he said, 'Everybody growing up or they leaving.'

Another time he said, 'I think I was a damn fool not to go and work with the Americans, like Edward and so much other people.'

Eddoes said, 'Hat going to town a lot these nights.'

Boyee said, 'Well, he is a big man. Why he shouldn't do what he want to do?'

Eddoes said, 'It have some men like that. As a matter of fact, it does happen to all man. They getting old and they get frighten and they want to remain young.'

I got angry with Eddoes because I didn't want to think of Hat in that way and the worst thing was that I was ashamed because I felt Eddoes was right.

I said, 'Eddoes, why you don't take your dirty mind somewhere else, eh? Why you don't leave all your dirtiness in the rubbish-dump?'

And then one day Hat brought home a woman.

I felt a little uneasy now in Hat's company. He had become a man with responsibility and obligations, and he could no longer give us all his time and attention. To make matters worse, everybody pretended that the woman wasn't there. Even Hat. He never spoke about her and he behaved as though he wanted us to believe that everything was just the same.

She was a pale-brown woman, about thirty, somewhat plump,

and her favourite colour was blue. She called herself Dolly. We used to see her looking blankly out of the windows of Hat's house. She never spoke to any of us. In fact, I hardly heard her speak at all, except to call Hat inside.

But Boyee and Edward were pleased with the changes she brought.

Boyee said, 'Is the first time I remember living with a woman in the house, and it make a lot of difference. Is hard to explain, but I find it nicer.'

My mother said, 'You see how man stupid. Hat see what happen to Edward and you mean to say that Hat still get hisself mix up with this woman?'

Mrs Morgan and Mrs Bhakcu saw so little of Dolly they had little to dislike in her, but they agreed that she was a lazy good-for-nothing.

Mrs Morgan said, 'This Dolly look like a old *madame* to me, you hear.'

It was easy enough for us to forget that Dolly was there, because Hat continued living as before. We still went to all the sports and we still sat on the pavement and talked.

Whenever Dolly piped, 'Hat, you coming?' Hat wouldn't reply.

About half an hour later Dolly would say, 'Hat, you coming or you ain't coming?'

And Hat would say then, 'I coming.'

I wondered what life was like for Dolly. She was nearly always inside the house and Hat was nearly always outside. She seemed to spend a great deal of her time at the front window looking out.

They were really the queerest couple in the street. They never went out together. We never heard them laughing. They never even quarrelled.

Eddoes said, 'They like two strangers.'

Errol said, 'Don't mind that, you hear. All you seeing Hat sitting quiet quiet here, but is different when he get inside. He ain't the same man when he talking with Dolly. He buy she a lot of joolry, you know.'

Eddoes said, 'I have a feeling she a little bit like Matilda. You know, the woman in the calypso:

> Matilda, Matilda,
> Matilda, you thief my money
> And gone Venezuela.

Buying joolry! But what happening to Hat? He behaving as though he is a old man. Woman don't want joolry from a man like Hat, they want something else.'

Looking on from the outside, though, one could see only two changes in Hat's household. All the birds were caged, and the Alsatian was chained and miserable.

But no one spoke about Dolly to Hat. I suppose the whole business had come as too much of a surprise.

What followed was an even bigger surprise, and it was some time before we could get all the details. At first I noticed Hat was missing, and then I heard rumours.

This was the story, as it later came out in court. Dolly had run away from Hat, taking all his gifts of course. Hat had chased her and found her with another man. There was a great quarrel, the man had fled, and Hat had taken it out on Dolly. Afterwards, the police statement said, he had gone, in tears, to the police station to give himself up. He said, 'I kill a woman.'

But Dolly wasn't dead.

We received the news as though it was news of a death. We couldn't believe it for a day or two.

And then a great hush fell on Miguel Street. No boys and men gathered under the lamp-post outside Hat's house, talking about this and that and the other. No one played cricket and disturbed people taking afternoon naps. The Club was dead.

Cruelly, we forgot all about Dolly and thought only about Hat.

We couldn't find it in our hearts to find fault with him. We suffered with him.

We saw a changed man in court. He had grown older, and when he smiled at us he smiled only with his mouth. Still, he put on a show for us and even while we laughed we were ready to cry.

The prosecutor asked Hat, 'Was it a dark night?'

Hat said, 'All night dark.'

Hat's lawyer was a short fat man called Chittaranjan who wore a smelly brown suit.

Chittaranjan began reeling off Portia's speech about mercy, and he would have gone on to the end if the judge hadn't said, 'All this is interesting and some of it even true but, Mr Chittaranjan, you are wasting the court's time.'

Chittaranjan made a great deal of fuss about the wild passion of love. He said Antony had thrown away an empire for the sake of love, just as Hat had thrown away his self-respect. He said that Hat's crime was really a *crime passionel*. In France, he said – and he knew what he was talking about, because he had been to Paris – in France, Hat would have been a hero. Women would have garlanded him.

Eddoes said, 'Is this sort of lawyer who does get man hang, you know.'

Hat was sentenced to four years.

We went to Frederick Street jail to see him. It was a disappointing jail. The walls were light cream, and not very high, and I was surprised to see that most of the visitors were very gay. Only a few women wept, but the whole thing was like a party, with people laughing and chatting.

Eddoes, who had put on his best suit for the occasion, held his hat in his hand and looked around. He said to Hat, 'It don't look too bad here.'

Hat said, 'They taking me to Carrera next week.'

Carrera was the small prison-island a few miles from Port of Spain.

Hat said, 'Don't worry about me. You know me. In two three weeks I go make them give me something easy to do.'

*

Whenever I went to Carenage or Point Cumana for a bathe, I looked across the green water to the island of Carrera, rising high out of the sea, with its neat pink buildings. I tried to picture what went on inside those buildings, but my imagination refused to work. I used to think, 'Hat there, I here. He know I here, thinking about him?'

But as the months passed I became more and more concerned with myself, and I wouldn't think about Hat for weeks on end. It was useless trying to feel ashamed. I had to face the fact that I was no longer missing Hat. From time to time when my mind was empty, I would stop and think how long it would be before he came out, but I was not really concerned.

I was fifteen when Hat went to jail and eighteen when he came out. A lot happened in those three years. I left school and I began working in the customs. I was no longer a boy. I was a man, earning money.

*

Hat's homecoming fell a little flat. It wasn't only that we boys had grown older. Hat too had changed. Some of the brightness had left him, and conversation was hard to make.

He visited all the houses he knew and he spoke about his experiences with great zest.

My mother gave him tea.

Hat said, 'Is just what I expect. I get friendly with some of the turnkey and them, and you know what happen? I pull two three strings and – bam! – they make me librarian. They have a big library there, you know. All sort of big book. Is the sort of place Titus Hoyt would like. So much book with nobody to read them.'

I offered Hat a cigarette and he took it mechanically.

Then he shouted, 'But, eh-eh, what is this? You come a big man now! When I leave you wasn't smoking. Was a long time now, though.'

I said, 'Yes. Was a long time.'

A long time. But it was just three years, three years in which I had grown up and looked critically at the people around me. I no longer wanted to be like Eddoes. He was so weak and thin, and I hadn't realized he was so small. Titus Hoyt was stupid and boring, and not funny at all. Everything had changed.

When Hat went to jail, part of me had died.

17. How I Left Miguel Street

My mother said, 'You getting too wild in this place. I think is high time you leave.'

'And go where? Venezuela?' I said.

'No, not Venezuela. Somewhere else, because the moment you land in Venezuela they go throw you in jail. I know you and I know Venezuela. No, somewhere else.'

I said, 'All right. You think about it and decide.'

My mother said, 'I go go and talk to Ganesh Pundit about it. He was a friend of your father. But you must go from here. You getting too wild.'

I suppose my mother was right. Without really knowing it, I had become a little wild. I was drinking like a fish, and doing a lot besides. The drinking started in the customs, where we confiscated liquor on the slightest pretext. At first the smell of the spirits upset me, but I used to say to myself, 'You must get over this. Drink it like medicine. Hold your nose and close your eyes.' In time I had become a first-class drinker, and I began suffering from drinker's pride.

Then there were the sights of the town Boyee and Errol introduced me to. One night, not long after I began working, they took me to a place near Marine Square. We climbed to the first floor and found ourselves in a small crowded room lit by green bulbs. The green light seemed as thick as jelly. There were many women all about the room, just waiting and looking. A big sign said: *Obscene Language Forbidden.*

We had a drink at the bar, a thick sweet drink.

Errol asked me, 'Which one of the women you like?'

I understood immediately, and I felt disgusted. I ran out of the room and went home, a little sick, a little frightened. I said to myself, 'You must get over this.'

Next night I went to the club again. And again.

We made wild parties and took rum and women to Maracas Bay for all-night sessions.

'You getting too wild,' my mother said.

I paid her no attention until the time I drank so much in one evening that I remained drunk for two whole days afterwards. When I sobered up, I made a vow neither to smoke nor drink again.

I said to my mother, 'Is not my fault really. Is just Trinidad. What else anybody can do here except drink?'

About two months later my mother said, 'You must come with me next week. We going to see Ganesh Pundit.'

Ganesh Pundit had given up mysticism for a long time. He had taken to politics and was doing very nicely. He was a minister of something or the other in the Government, and I heard people saying that he was in the running for the M.B.E.

We went to his big house in St Clair and we found the great man, not dressed in *dhoti* and *koortah*, as in the mystic days, but in an expensive-looking lounge suit.

He received my mother with a good deal of warmth.

He said, 'I do what I could do.'

My mother began to cry.

To me Ganesh said, 'What you want to go abroad to study?'

I said, 'I don't want to study anything really. I just want to go away, that's all.'

Ganesh smiled and said, 'The Government not giving away

that sort of scholarship yet. Only ministers could do what you say. No, you have to study something.'

I said, 'I never think about it really. Just let me think a little bit.'

Ganesh said, 'All right. You think a little bit.'

My mother was crying her thanks to Ganesh.

I said, 'I know what I want to study. Engineering.' I was thinking about my uncle Bhakcu.

Ganesh laughed and said, 'What *you* know about engineering?'

I said, 'Right now, nothing. But I could put my mind to it.'

My mother said, 'Why don't you want to take up law?'

I thought of Chittaranjan and his brown suit and I said, 'No, not law.'

Ganesh said, 'It have only one scholarship remaining. For drugs.'

I said, 'But I don't want to be a druggist. I don't want to put on a white jacket and sell lipstick to woman.'

Ganesh smiled.

My mother said, 'You mustn't mind the boy. Pundit. He will study drugs.' And to me, 'You could study anything if you put your mind to it.'

Ganesh said, 'Think. It mean going to London. It mean seeing snow and seeing the Thames and seeing the big Parliament.'

I said, 'All right. I go study drugs.'

My mother said, 'I don't know what I could do to thank you, Pundit.'

And, crying, she counted out two hundred dollars and gave it to Ganesh. She said, 'I know it ain't much, Pundit. But is all I have. Is a long time I did saving it up.'

Ganesh took the money sadly and he said, 'You mustn't let that worry you. You must give only what you can afford.'

My mother kept on crying and in the end even Ganesh broke down.

When my mother saw this, she dried her tears and said, 'If you only know, Pundit, how worried I is. I have to find so much money for so much thing these days, and I don't really know how I going to make out.'

Ganesh now stopped crying. My mother began to cry afresh.

This went on for a bit until Ganesh gave back a hundred dollars to my mother. He was sobbing and shaking and he said, 'Take this and buy some good clothes for the boy.'

I said, 'Pundit, you is a good man.'

This affected him strongly. He said, 'Is when you come back from England, with all sort of certificate and paper, a big man and a big druggist, is then I go come round and ask you for what you owe me.'

I told Hat I was going away.

He said, 'What for? Labouring?'

I said, 'The Government give me a scholarship to study drugs.'

He said, 'Is you who wangle that?'

I said, 'Not me. My mother.'

Eddoes said, 'Is a good thing. A druggist fellow I know – picking up rubbish for him for years now – this fellow rich like anything. Man, the man just rolling in money.'

The news got to Elias and he took it badly. He came to the gate one evening and shouted, 'Bribe, bribe. Is all you could do. Bribe.'

My mother shouted back. 'The only people who does complain about bribe is those who too damn poor to have anything to bribe with.'

In about a month everything was fixed for my departure. The Trinidad Government wrote to the British Consul in New York about me. The British Council got to know about me. The Americans gave me a visa after making me swear that I wouldn't overthrow their government by armed force.

The night before I left, my mother gave a little party. It was something like a wake. People came in looking sad and telling me how much they were going to miss me, and then they forgot about me and attended to the serious business of eating and drinking.

Laura kissed me on the cheek and gave me a medallion of St Christopher. She asked me to wear it around my neck. I promised that I would and put the medallion in my pocket. I don't know what happened to it. Mrs Bhakcu gave me a sixpenny piece which she said she had had specially consecrated. It didn't look different from other sixpenny pieces and I suppose I spent it. Titus Hoyt forgave me everything and brought me Volume Two of the Everyman edition of Tennyson. Eddoes gave me a wallet which he swore was practically new. Boyee and Errol gave me nothing. Hat gave me a carton of cigarettes. He said, 'I know you say you ain't smoking again. But take this, just in case you change your mind.' The result was that I began smoking again.

Uncle Bhakcu spent the night fixing the van which was to take me to the airport next morning. From time to time I ran out and begged him to take it easy. He said he thought the carburettor was playing the fool.

Next morning Bhakcu got up early and was at it again. We had planned to leave at eight, but at ten to, Bhakcu was still tinkering. My mother was in a panic and Mrs Bhakcu was growing impatient.

Bhakcu was underneath the car, whistling a couplet from the *Ramayana*. He came out, laughed, and said, 'You getting frighten, eh?'

Presently we were all ready. Bhakcu had done little damage to the engine and it still worked. My bags were taken to the van and I was ready to leave the house for the last time.

My mother said, 'Wait.'

She placed a brass jar of milk in the middle of the gateway.

I cannot understand, even now, how it happened. The gateway was wide, big enough for a car, and the jar, about four inches wide, was in the middle. I thought I was walking at the edge of the gateway, far away from the jar. And yet I kicked the jar over.

My mother's face fell.

I said, 'Is a bad sign?'

She didn't answer.

Bhakcu was blowing the horn.

We got into the van and Bhakcu drove away, down Miguel Street and up Wrightson Road to South Quay. I didn't look out of the windows.

My mother was crying. She said, 'I know I not going to ever see you in Miguel Street again.'

I said, 'Why? Because I knock the milk down?'

She didn't reply, still crying for the spilt milk.

Only when we had left Port of Spain and the suburbs I looked outside. It was a clear, hot day. Men and women were working in rice-fields. Some children were bathing under a stand-pipe at the side of the road.

We got to Piarco in good time, and at this stage I began wishing I had never got the scholarship. The airport lounge frightened me. Fat Americans were drinking strange drinks at the bar. American women, wearing haughty sun-glasses, raised their voices whenever they spoke. They all looked too rich, too comfortable.

Then the news came, in Spanish and English. Flight 206 had been delayed for six hours.

I said to my mother, 'Let we go back to Port of Spain.'

I had to be with those people in the lounge soon anyway, and I wanted to put off the moment.

And back in Miguel Street the first person I saw was Hat. He was strolling flat-footedly back from the café, with a paper under his arm. I waved and shouted at him.

All he said was, 'I thought you was in the air by this time.'

I was disappointed. Not only by Hat's cool reception. Disappointed because although I had been away, destined to be gone for good, everything was going on just as before, with nothing to indicate my absence.

I looked at the overturned brass jar in the gateway and I said to my mother, 'So this mean I was never going to come back here, eh?'

She laughed and looked happy.

So I had my last lunch at home, with my mother and Uncle Bhakcu and his wife. Then back along the hot road to Piarco where the plane was waiting. I recognized one of the customs' officers, and he didn't check my baggage.

The announcement came, a cold, casual thing.

I embraced my mother.

I said to Bhakcu, 'Uncle Bhak, I didn't want to tell you before, but I think I hear your tappet knocking.'

His eyes shone.

I left them all and walked briskly towards the aeroplane, not looking back, looking only at my shadow before me, a dancing dwarf on the tarmac.

picador.com

blog
videos
interviews
extracts